HERE COMES THE BRIDESMAID

BY
L TREMAYNE

MILLS & BOON

First published in Great Britain 2014
by Mills & Boon, an imprint of Harlequin (UK) Limited,
Eton House, 18-24 Paradise Road, Richmond, Surrey, TW9 1SR

ISBN: 978-0-263-24278-2

Harlequin (UK) Limited's policy is to use papers that are natural,
renewable and recyclable products and made from wood grown in
sustainable forests. The logging and manufacturing processes conform
to the legal environmental regulations of the country of origin.

Printed and bound in Great Britain
by CPI Antony Rowe, Chippenham, Wiltshire

'And could I have a Campari and soda while I wait for my friend?'

'Fine,' Leo said, irritated. 'I'll get one sent over.'

'And—'

'Good God, what else?'

'Just that it's Gary's birthday. So if there's a special dessert or something…?'

'Yes. I. Will. Send. Out. A. Special. Dessert. Now, are you all right for socks and undies, or do you need me to get you some of those too?'

'Actually, I never wear socks.' Sunshine smiled serenely. 'And I'm not wearing undies tonight—not under *this* dress!'

Leo could feel his eyes bug out of his head. 'Thanks for that mental picture, Sunshine. Anything else you'd care to share?'

'Well…'

'Yeah, hold that thought,' he said, and made a bolt for the kitchen. Where he leaned against the wall and burst out laughing.

His sous chef looked at him as if he'd grown a gigantic unicorn horn.

Clearly it had been a long time since he'd laughed.

Dear Reader

Food is a great passion of mine—in fact I'm in love with about a dozen celebrity chefs. So I wasn't exactly surprised to find myself becoming fixated on the idea of a chef as a hero…and Leo Quartermaine was born.

My other great passion is shoes. Oh, my goodness, the *shoes*! So…hello, Sunshine Smart.

And, of course, I'm partial to a nice romantic wedding.

HERE COMES THE BRIDESMAID gave me a chance to combine all three things in a setting always irresistible to me—my hometown, Sydney—as best man Leo and bridesmaid Sunshine are put in charge of planning the perfect wedding for two absent grooms.

Leo is driven, grumpy and serious. Sunshine is quirky, perky and enthusiastic. They have different takes on love, on life, on relationships—not exactly the easiest working combination to plan a wedding reception. Add in an inconvenient sexual attraction, and things get even trickier.

But HERE COMES THE BRIDESMAID is more than a story about opposites attracting—although the clash of personalities in Sunshine and Leo's case *can* lead to some eye-popping conversations! It's also about being jolted out of your comfort zone and opening yourself to everything that's in you, and finding the one you thought you'd never find—ready-or-not-here-I-come.

And there's nothing quite as romantic as being taken by surprise by love.

I hope you enjoy HERE COMES THE BRIDESMAID.

Avril Tremayne

XXXX

Avril Tremayne read *Jane Eyre* as a teenager and has been hooked on tales of passion and romance ever since. An opportunistic insomniac, she has been a lifelong crazy-mad reader, but she took the scenic route to becoming a writer—via gigs as diverse as shoe salesgirl, hot cross bun packer, teacher, and public relations executive. She has spent a good chunk of her life travelling, and has more favourite destinations than should be strictly allowable.

Avril is happily settled in her hometown of Sydney, Australia, where her husband and daughter try to keep her out of trouble—not always successfully. When she's not writing or reading she can generally be found eating—although she does *not* cook!

Check out her website, www.avriltremayne.com, or follow her on Twitter, @AvrilTremayne, and Facebook, www.facebook.com/avril.tremayne

HERE COMES THE BRIDESMAID
is Avril Tremayne's debut book
for Modern Tempted™!

This title is also available in eBook format
from www.millsandboon.co.uk

Dedicated, with thanks, to my husband and @kder
for absolutely everything.

To the astute, eagle-eyed Americans Lisa McNair Palmer
and Melinda Wirth for knowing what's good
and what's definitely not.

And to each and every one of my marriage-minded friends!

CHAPTER ONE

TO: Jonathan Jones
FROM: Sunshine Smart
SUBJECT: Bridesmaid meets Best Man
Darling Jon
I've met Leo and I adore him!

We are on the same page, so fear not—your wedding reception will be everything you ever dreamed of!

Wish we could have the actual marriage in Sydney too, but hooray for enlightened New York!

Hugs and kisses to Caleb.
Sunny xxx

TO: Caleb Quartermaine
FROM: Leo Quartermaine
SUBJECT: WTF??????
Caleb
What are you doing to me?

Sunshine Smart cannot be a real name. And she wants to friend me on Facebook! NOT JOKING!

Despite being dropped in it with the lunatic, I will ensure the dinner doesn't turn into a three-ring circus.

Can't wait to meet Jonathan—but please tell me he's nothing like his bridesmaid.
LQ

SUNSHINE SMART WAS looking forward to her second meeting with Leo Quartermaine. *Despite* their introductory meeting two days ago, lasting just ten minutes and ending with him declining her request to be Facebook friends.

She loved Leo's restaurants—well, what she'd read about them. Because she'd never actually eaten at one... which she was about to remedy.

She loved him on TV—tough but fair, judging those reality TV would-be chefs, and *dreamy as* when fronting *Cook It Up With Leo.*

She was predisposed to love anyone whose brother was smart enough to marry her best friend Jonathan Jones.

And she just—well, *loved* him. In that *Isn't he adorable?* way of loving people who were just so solid and serious and a teensy bit repressed.

But his hair—or lack thereof—was a problem. There was no *reason* for Leo to shave his head. It wasn't as if he had a comb-over issue. He could have a full head of hair if he wanted! Lush, thick, wheat-blond. She'd seen the 'before shaved head' photos on the internet. And the start of the regrowth at their first meeting. She'd read a comment in an article about it being easier in the kitchen without hair—but she wasn't asking for a ponytail!

Anyway, that could be fixed. There was time for him to grow it. She would just drop a word in his ear.

Sunshine checked her make-up. Her new red lipstick looked fabulous. Her eyes...well, what could you do? The grey eyeshadow was heavily layered; mascara so thick each lash look like a tarantula leg—make-up intended to distract people from her ocular weirdness. About which there was nothing she could do—unlike Leo Quartermaine's hair!

She got out of her car—a bright yellow 1970s relic— and walked purposefully towards Q Brasserie.

* * *

Leo Quartermaine heard Sunshine approach before he saw her.

He associated that tap-tapping rhythm on the polished concrete floor with her, despite only having met her once before.

He was betting she was wearing another pair of ankle-breaking high heels.

To be fair, she *was* a shoe designer. But shoe designers made flats, didn't they? Like those ballet-slipper things. Not that he could picture Sunshine Smart in ballet slippers. Or trainers—crikey!

'Leo!' she called out, as though he were a misplaced winning lottery ticket, suddenly found. He was starting to think 'ecstatic' was her default setting.

'Sunshine,' he said, managing not to roll his eyes. *Sunshine!* How had her parents put that on the birth certificate without gagging?

'So!'

He'd already clocked the fact that she often started her utterances with 'So!' As though an amazing revelation would be out of her mouth on the next breath.

'News!' she said, tap-tapping towards the window table where he was sitting.

And, yep, six inches of spike on her feet. In electric blue patent leather. God help his eyes.

She stripped off her trench coat as she made her way across the floor, causing her long necklace to swing. He'd noticed the necklace last time. Pretty. Three types of gold—a rose gold chain, with a yellow gold sun and white gold moon dangling from it.

Miraculously, her dress was an understated colour— pale grey-blue. But it fitted her like a second skin and had one of those things—pellums? Peplums? Whatever!—that dragged a man's eyes to a woman's waist and hips. She had a hell of a figure, he had to admit. Curvaceous, like the hourglass pin-up girls of the 1950s.

Leo got up to pull out a chair for her on the opposite side of the table. She took the opportunity to kiss him on the cheek, party-girl air-kiss style—except it wasn't like any air-kiss he'd ever had—and he'd had plenty. It was a smacking, relishing kiss. *Not* the kind of kiss to slap on a person you barely knew.

Oblivious to his momentary shock, Sunshine tossed her trench coat carelessly onto a nearby chair, sat, and beamed up at him. 'Did you hear? They've set the date. October twentieth. So we've got two months. A spring wedding. Yay!'

Yay? Who the hell said 'yay'? Leo returned to his seat. 'Not much time, but doable.'

'Oh, it's *oodles* of time,' Sunshine assured him airily. 'So! I've made a list of everything we need to do, and now we can decide who does what, give each task a deadline, and go from there.'

'List?' Leo repeated the word, apprehensive. He liked lists. He worked well with lists. The haphazard approach to life of his wastrel and usually wast*ed* parents had made him a plan-crazy list junkie. But this was a simple dinner he could organise with his eyes closed while he whisked a chocolate soufflé.

For once in his life he *didn't* need a list.

'Yes.' She reached down beside her to where she'd dumped the silver leather bag she'd been swinging when she walked over and pulled out a dazzling chartreuse folder. She removed some paper, peeled off two pages and held them out to him. 'Your copy. I'm actually not really into lists,' she confessed—*surprise, surprise*. 'So it may need some work.'

He looked at the first page. At the big, bold heading: *The Marriage Celebration of Jonathan and Caleb, October 20th.*

Seeing the words was like a punch to the solar plexus. It was real. Happening. Imminent. His baby brother was getting married.

What were the odds? Two Aussie guys who'd never met in their own country moved separately to New York, met at a random party, and—bang!—happy-ever-after.

It didn't matter that Leo didn't know Jonathan, because Jonathan made Caleb happy. It didn't matter that the ceremony was taking place on the other side of the world, because the place was just logistics. It didn't matter that their marriage was only going to be legally recognised in a handful of countries, because *they* knew what it meant wherever they were.

Leo wondered if he would have had more luck meeting the love of his life if *he* were gay. Because it sure wasn't happening for him on his side of the sexuality fence. The succession of glossy glamour-pusses who seemed to be the only women that came his way were certainly lovely to look at—but they didn't *eat*, and they didn't occupy his thoughts for longer than it took to produce a mutual orgasm.

He wanted what Caleb had. The one. Someone to get into his head, under his skin, to intrigue and dazzle and delight him. Someone who burrowed into his core instead of bouncing off his shell. Someone to belong to. And to belong to him.

He thought back to his last failure—beautiful, talented singing sensation Natalie Clarke. She'd told him on their second date that she loved him. But nobody fell in love in two dates! Nope—what she'd loved was the concept of Leo the celebrity chef. She'd wanted them to be part of 'the scene'. And who said *'the scene'* with a straight face? He couldn't think of anything worse than 'the scene'…except maybe her predilection for snorting cocaine, because apparently *everyone* on *'the scene'* did it.

In any case, she was a relentless salad-with-dressing-on-the-side type. And she liked playing her own cheesy love songs in the bedroom *way* too much.

With a repressed shudder he brought his mind back to the present and ran his eyes down the list.

Budget
Wedding Party
Master of Ceremonies
Venue
Menu
Alcohol
Guest List
Invitations
Flowers
Lighting
Music
Cake
Clothing
Shoes
Hair and Make-up

What the hell…? Why did *that* need a subheading?

Gift Registry
Photographer
Videographer
Wedding Favours
Order of Proceedings
Toasts and Speeches
Printing
Seating Plan

Each item was bullet-pointed with a little box that could be ticked, and accompanied by questions, comments and suggestions.

Good thing she wasn't into lists!

Sunshine must have noticed the stunned look on Leo's face, because she asked, 'Have I screwed it up?'

'This is...' he started, but words actually failed him.

'Exciting?' Sunshine suggested, looking as if she were about to celebrate Christmas, her birthday *and* the wedding all at once.

'Comprehensive,' Leo corrected. He ran a hand across his scalp. Her eyes followed his hand. She was frowning suddenly. He wondered what was going through her mind.

She opened her mouth. Closed it. Opened it. Closed it. Sighed.

Then, 'So!' she said. 'The venue is the first thing. Because it's bound to be tricky, securing somewhere wonderful with only two months' notice.'

'It may have escaped your notice, but I am a restaurateur,' Leo said. 'I *have* venues. I *am* venues. *And* menus. And *booze*.'

Sunshine seemed startled. 'Oh. I just assumed we'd be too late to get a large group booked into one of your places. That's why I've suggested somewhere like the hotel on—'

'My brother is *not* celebrating his marriage in a hotel.'

'Okay. Well, there's that lovely place that used to be a stately home in—'

'Or in an old house.'

'Then perhaps the new convention space—which is not as tragic as it sounds. In fact it has a—'

He slammed his hand on the table. 'No!' He stopped, reined in the spurt of annoyance. 'No.' *Better. Calmer.* 'We have a perfectly...' *Reaching, reaching...* 'Perfectly perfect...' *hmm, thesaurus required* '...private room in this restaurant.'

The only sign that Sunshine had noted his ill-tempered hand-banging incoherence was a tiny twitch at one side of her mouth. He feared—he really feared—she was trying not to laugh.

'Which seats…?' she asked, her head on one side like a bird, with every indication of deep interest.

'Seats?'

'How many people does the private room seat?'

'Twenty-five.'

Sunshine crossed her arms—seemingly unaware of how she was framing her rather spectacular breasts—and looked at him, apologetic. 'See? Me and lists! I got the order wrong. "Guest List" should have come before "Venue". So! Let's take a step back. I have Jon's invitation list. Do you have Caleb's?'

'It's coming today some time.'

'Because there are seventy-five people on our side.'

He stared. 'You are not serious.'

'I assure you, I am. And that's with a savage cull.' She shuddered theatrically as she uncrossed her arms. *'Savage.'*

'Caleb wants an intimate dinner.'

'That's not my understanding, but I'll tell you what—you check with Caleb overnight, and we can reconvene tomorrow.'

His eyes narrowed. 'I hate it when people try to soothe me.'

Sunshine bit her lip. 'Oh, dear, and I was *trying* to sound like I was keeping an open mind. But…okay. I'll tell you straight out, if you prefer: there is no way this is going to be a dinner for twenty-five people. And there's no use getting in a snit about it—it's just the way it is.'

'I'm not in a snit.'

'If you say so.'

'I do. Say so.'

'All right.'

'I'm *not.*'

'All *right.*'

Another mouth-twitch. She was *definitely* trying not to laugh.

And Leo had had enough. 'I have to go,' he said, despite not being needed in the kitchen for fifteen minutes.

'Yes, I can see everything's getting under way here. I love the buzz of restaurants. Jon and I used to try a new restaurant every other week. I miss him. He's so...so important to me.' Her voice wobbled the merest fraction as she added the last bit.

Uh-oh, tears. Leo didn't do tears. He felt himself shrink back. Wanted to run.

But her face morphed into something tortured, right before his eyes, and he froze. It was as if a layer had been ripped off her in one half-second. Her eyes were strained and yet also vacant, as if she were seeing...emptiness. Her lips trembled. Her skin looked ashen. Every trace of happiness was obliterated. The contrast with her normal exuberance was dramatic—almost painful to see.

All this because her best friend had moved overseas and she missed him?

Huh?

Leo wanted to touch her. Pat her hand or...something. Say...something. He who never touched, never comforted, because he didn't know how. His hands fisted uselessly.

Then Sunshine blinked. Shook her head—tiny, tiny movement. And in another half-second everything clicked back to normal and Leo breathed a silent sigh of relief.

'Um...' he said. Yep, he was super-articulate today.

But she was smiling blindingly, as though that moment had never happened, so he did the sensible thing and shut up.

'We haven't got far down the list,' she said. 'What about if I shortcircuit a few things? You know, invitations, et cetera.'

'What do you mean, "shortcircuit"? And "et cetera"?'

he asked, still a little shaken. Everything about her was throwing him off kilter.

'I'll get some options together for us to look over tomorrow. Nothing scary!'

She was completely back to normal. Full-strength perky. Better than the tragic facemask she'd freaked him out with—but only marginally. Leo didn't like perky. And if he were being made to board Sunshine Smart's good ship *Lollipop* for this wedding *he* would be the one at the tiller.

'I thought we'd be emailing the invitations,' he said.

She gave him what could only be termed a pitying smile. 'Did you?'

That was all. She wasn't even going to bother arguing.

Um...no. That was not how it was going to work. 'It's the twenty-first century,' he said. 'And time is short. I've seen some brilliant cutting-edge online invitations.'

'Well, why don't you bring one of those examples to our meeting tomorrow on your tablet/device/notebook/whatever you've got, and I'll bring some hard copy snail mail samples appropriate for a chic but traditional wedding celebration.'

'You're doing the soothe thing again.'

'Oh, dear, am I? I'll have to work on that,' she said.

It was obvious to Leo that she had no intention of doing anything of the sort. But he wasn't going to waste his breath pointing that out. He was tired enough from just *looking* at her.

'We'll talk tomorrow—*after* I've checked with Caleb,' he said shortly, and stood abruptly.

'Just one more thing, Leo, before you rush off.'

He looked down at her and she cleared her throat.

'What?' Leo asked, trying not to feel a sense of impending doom.

'Just...something that's going to have to start now, like right this second, if it's going to be ready in two months.'

'And are you going to share with me exactly what this all-important thing is?'

'Promise you won't get mad?'

'No.'

'It's important.'

'Waiting.'

'I wouldn't ask if it wasn't absolutely vital. It's just…' She stopped, ran her hand through her long hair, widened her eyes at him as though she were trying to impart something telepathically. Ran her hand through her hair again.

And he—

God! The eyes. Why hadn't he noticed her eyes before?

She huffed out a breath and pursed her lips. Exasperated because he hadn't read her chaotic mind, probably.

But all he could think about were her eyes.

'Hair,' she explained. 'It only grows one-point-two-five centimetres a month. One-point-three if you're lucky.'

'So?'

'You have to start growing your hair.'

He had no answer. Might well have been gaping like a hooked fish.

'Sorry—but if I didn't raise it now you might have shaved your head tonight and it would be a shame to lose those few millimetres.'

'I don't want to grow my hair,' Leo said. Ultra-reasonable. The way you talked to a person who was certifiably insane.

'But you will look so much better in the photos. And you have lovely hair.'

'And you know this…how?'

'I looked you up online and saw the photos from the launch of this place, when you had hair. Now, I'm not saying you're not very good-looking even *with* the shaved head. Tall, but not in a carnival freaky way. Lean—which is amazing, for a chef, if you ask me. Wonderful sharp cheekbones, brilliant smile— All right, I'm guessing the smile bit, since I haven't actually seen it, but I'm a good guesser. And really lovely eyes—amber is such an unusual colour, you know? Tigerish. But if you look quite delectable now, you will be absolutely, irresistibly *gorgeous* with hair.'

Leo stood there, gobsmacked. 'I've got to get to work,' he said when he could trust himself to speak.

'But you'll think about the hair, won't you?' she asked anxiously. 'And while you're thinking, maybe keep the razor off your scalp…just in case you *do* decide to look absolutely, irresistibly *gorgeous* at your brother's wedding.'

He looked at her. Noted her eyes again. Really stunning eyes. *She* would look absolutely, irresistibly gorgeous herself if she—

Aha.

Leo could have crowed, he was so pleased with himself. 'Let's make a deal—you go into the bathroom and wash off that eye-goop right now, and I will not shave my head…unless I see that crap all over your eyes again. The minute I see it, I'm reaching for the razor.'

And, yes! He'd stumped her. She was the gaping fish now.

He watched as she processed what he'd said. She lifted her bag off the floor and rummaged inside, pulled out a compact. Flipped it open, looked in the mirror. Widened her eyes, then squinted. Turned her head to peer sideways, then switched sides and did it again. 'You know that I have strange eyes, right?' she asked.

'Beautiful eyes.'

'Evil eyes.'

'Yeah, maybe lay off the sci-fi.'

'Oh, it's a real condition. It's called heterochromia iridum, and there are various theories about how you get it. Genetics, melanin levels, trauma, chimerism—which is kind of creepy because it means another foetus has merged with you in the womb, which in my case would mean there were initially three of us, because— Well, anyway, I don't like the idea of absorbing a sibling in the womb—hello, Dr Frankenstein!' Pause for breath. 'All that aside, I'm pretty sure they used to burn people like me at the stake as witches back in the day.'

'Nobody is going to burn you at the stake in modern-day Australia for having one blue and one green eye.'

'I've tried contact lenses, but there is nothing that makes you panic quite like a contact lens that's slipped up under your eyelid and you think it's going to be there for eternity unless you race off to the emergency room and have someone stick some implement in there against your poor squishy eyeball. Talk about bloodshot!' She pursed her lips. 'But I guess I could try them again—maybe some amber ones.' She looked into his eyes, considering. 'Because your eyes really are lovely, and I think I'd look kind of interesting with amber eyes.'

'You do that and I'm shaving my head.'

Sunshine took another look in the mirror, then snapped the compact shut. 'All right. Deal. I may need a little make-up on the actual day of the reception, just so I don't look Plain Janerama, but no camouflage paint in the meantime. I'm keeping the lipstick, though—I can't go completely naked. So! Where's the bathroom?'

Plain Janerama? Leo, speechless, pointed.

Sunshine got to her feet. 'No need to wait,' she told him.

'Oh, I'm waiting.'

She squared her shoulders. 'This is going to be *weird*,' she said, and tap-tapped away.

Leo checked that everything was in order in the kitchen, then returned to the table. He went through the checklist again. Swore under his breath. He suspected Sunshine Smart usually got her way in all things. Which meant she was in for a surprise, because just on principle he wasn't going to let that happen. He hadn't got where he was today by doing what people told him. His survival instinct told him always to go his *own* way, to *get* his own way.

He started jotting down menu ideas—appropriate for a dinner for twenty-five people—but hadn't got far when he heard the tap-tap of Sunshine's returning high heels.

She plonked herself into the chair opposite and did an over-the-top eyelash-bat at him.

Leo stared at her. He couldn't help it. Without the exaggerated eye make-up she looked fresh and clean and sweet as suckable candy. Her dark chocolate hair against the ultra-white skin of her face seemed more dramatic. With the edge of her heavy fringe now damp and misplaced, he could see how fine and dark her eyebrows were, and that they arched intriguingly towards the outer edge. Her eyelashes were thick and black enough to form a fine line around her eyes. And her eyes were simply spectacular. Heavy-lidded, slightly tilted, the colour difference so dramatic without the dark shadow and over-clumped lashes that he couldn't seem to stop looking at them.

'Well?' she asked, batting away.

'Better,' Leo said, with impressive understatement. He got to his feet. 'I'll see you tomorrow, then—an hour earlier, if you can make it. But you'll have to come to Mainefare—it's in the Pig and Poke pub. Do you know it?'

'Yes, I know it—and, yes, that's fine. But before you go can I ask just one more favour?'

Leo eyed her suspiciously.

'I'm staying for dinner,' she explained. 'Don't worry— I have a booking. It's just that my date—Gary, his name is—is a massive foodie, and he'd really love to meet you. Perhaps you could just pop out and say hello…?'

'Oh, sure,' Leo agreed easily. He'd been expecting something worse—maybe that he have a shot of Botox!—

and, anyway, speaking to his customers was part of his routine.

'And do you think I could have this exact table? It has a lovely view over the park. If it's reserved I'll understand, but—'

He caught his impatient sigh before it could erupt. 'You can have the table, Sunshine.'

'And could I have a Campari and soda while I wait for Gary?'

'Fine,' Leo said, irritated that it made him curious about her—because he would have pegged her for a Cosmopolitan girl. And who the hell *cared* what she liked to drink? 'I'll get one sent over.'

'And—'

'Good God, what else?'

'Just that it's Gary's birthday…so if there's a special dessert or something…?'

'Yes. I. Will. Send. Out. A. Special. Dessert. Now, are you all right for socks and undies, or do you need me to get you some of those too?'

'Actually, I never wear socks.' Sunshine smiled serenely. 'And I'm not wearing undies tonight—not under *this* dress!'

Leo could feel his eyes bug out of his head. 'Thanks for that mental picture, Sunshine. Anything else you'd care to share?'

'Well…'

'Yeah, hold that thought,' he said, and made a bolt for the kitchen. Where he leant against the wall and burst out laughing.

His sous chef looked at him as if he'd grown a gigantic unicorn horn.

Clearly it had been a long time since he'd laughed.

Yum.

That was the word that had been popping into Sun-

shine's head with monotonous regularity from the moment
Leo had sent out a bowl of polenta chips with a gorgonzola
dipping sauce to snack on while she drank her Campari.

Q Brasserie had an open kitchen, so she could not only
smell but also see the magic being wrought on an array
of seafood and meat—and, okay, vegetables too, although
they were a lot less interesting if you asked her.

She rubbernecked as a steady stream of mouthwater-
ing dishes was whisked past her en route to other diners,
agonised over the menu choices and wished she could eat
everything.

Sunshine basically Hoovered up her entrée of six plump,
perfectly sautéed scallops, served with a Japanese-style
dressing of cucumber, rice vinegar, mirin, and ginger. And
it took great willpower *not* to beg a taste of Gary's mush-
rooms with truffle custard. She wouldn't normally covet
a vegetarian dish but, come on, truffle custard? *Yum!*

The main meals were sublime. She ate every bite of
her Angus beef brisket, served with smoked bone mar-
row and potato confit, and, giving in to her inner piglet
on the date-taste issue, was in the process of polishing off
one of Gary's divine king prawns—chargrilled with coriander and lime, *yum, yum, yum*—when up bowled Leo.

He'd changed from his jeans, T-shirt and way cool
brown leather lace-ups into a spotlessly clean, double-
breasted chef's jacket, finely checked pants and classy
black slip-ons, and he looked sigh-worthy.

Leo looked at her well-cleaned plate. At Gary's. At the
tiny piece of prawn on the end of her fork. His eyebrows
shot up.

Sunshine knew she was presenting as a glutton—but
so what? She liked food! Sue her! She calmly finished the
last bite of prawn and laid her fork on her plate.

She made the introductions, then retreated as Leo en-
gaged Gary in a conversation about food.

Gary looked a little starstruck. Which was kind of sweet. *He* was kind of sweet. Not that their relationship was going anywhere. This was their third date and from her perspective he'd settled into purely platonic material. She hadn't had even one lascivious thought about him.

The conversation moved on from food and Gary was explaining a little about his job. He was an investment banker—which was more interesting than it sounded. Truly!

'Nice talking to you Gary,' Leo said eventually. 'Dessert is on the house. Happy birthday, and enjoy the rest of your evening.'

Leo had been aware of Sunshine beaming her approval all through his talk with Gary. It was irritating, like a tiny pebble stuck in your shoe, to have her there—just there… just…*there*. Like a hyped-up Miss Congeniality.

In fact the whole evening had been irritating, because that damned table he'd pinched from one of his regulars was in his line of sight from the kitchen, so he'd been in Peeping Tom mode all night. Watching as she ate. And ate and ate. As she made Gary laugh. And laugh and laugh.

Gary was clearly besotted with her. Poor guy. He was handsome—a nice man—but not in Sunshine's league. Not that Leo knew what Sunshine's league *was*, only that Gary wasn't in it. Which had been underscored by the expression on Sunshine's face when the Persian nougat glacé had arrived at the table. The way her glowing eyes had closed as she took the first bite, then opened as the taste hit her. How her mouth had oozed over the spoon…

And why hadn't he noticed the shape of her mouth before? Too much coloured gunk, he supposed. But once the lipstick had worn off she hadn't bothered reapplying it. Which was odd, wasn't it? He'd never known a girl *not* to race off and reapply her lipstick *ad nauseam* during dinner.

Not that Sunshine's lipstick habits were any of his business.

Except that now he couldn't miss her too-heavy top lip, glistening as she darted her tongue over it. The wide and chewable bottom lip. She had a little gap between her two front teeth that was kooky-meets-adorable. And she moved her mouth over her spoon as if she were having a food-induced orgasm.

He wondered if he was thinking in orgasm terms because she was going commando tonight. *Not* that he was going there. No way! *And please, God, get the thought out of my head!*

Whatever, she'd clearly appreciated the 2002 Cristal her boyfriend had ordered to go with dessert.

Leo preferred the 1996 vintage.

Talk about splitting hairs. What the hell was wrong with him?

He sighed. Stretched. It had been a long night, that was all. He just needed to get to bed. Right after he emailed Caleb. He was going to get the dinner party back under control at their meeting tomorrow. Put Sunshine the Bulldozer back in the shed.

Sunshine. *Groan!* She was like a six-inch electric blue thorn in his side.

So it didn't make sense that he would be humming as he thought about that manifesto-sized checklist of hers.

And damn if it wasn't that cheesy Natalie Clarke number about love biting you in the ass.

The most diabolically awful song of the century.

Clearly, he needed a drink.

God, he hated Barry White.

CHAPTER TWO

TO: Caleb Quartermaine
FROM: Leo Quartermaine
SUBJECT: Seriously?
Caleb, mate

What's the deal? Where's your invitation list? Are we really talking 150 guests? I thought it was an intimate dinner.

Sunshine is descending on me tomorrow to kick off the invitation process, so it would be nice to know who's got what expectations. So I don't end up looking like a completely clueless moron.

LQ

TO: Jonathan Jones
FROM: Sunshine Smart
SUBJECT: Wedding of the century
Hello, darling

Had dinner at Q Brasserie tonight—fabulous. We're meeting again at one of Leo's other places, Mainefare, tomorrow. Can't wait!

I've worked out that Mainefare is a play on words. Mayfair as in London (it's in a British-style pub) but with Maine as in Quartermaine and fare as in food. Leo is so clever!

Invitation samples attached: (1) ultra-modern, cream and charcoal; (2) dreamy romantic in mauve and violet;

(3) Art Deco—blue and teal with yellow, brown, and grey accents.

PLEASE like the Art Deco one, which I know sounds ghastly, but open it and you'll see!

All else is on track. Party of the year, I'm telling you! Sunny xxx

PS—and, no, in answer to your repeat question—I have not done it yet. You're getting as bad as Mum and Dad.

TAP-TAP-TAP. Same sound effect, just on floorboards.

Leo saw her scan the room. Mainefare wasn't as open as Q Brasserie and it was harder to spot people—so he stood, waved.

His eyes went automatically to Sunshine's feet. Coral suede. Maybe four inches high—he figured the missing inches equalled casual for her. Oddly, no polish on her toenails; now that he thought of it, he hadn't seen colour on her toenails at their previous two meetings. Finger-nails either.

Hello, Mr Estee Lauder—since when do you start no-ticing nail polish?

He *didn't*. Of course he didn't. But she just looked like the kind of girl who wouldn't be seen dead with unpainted nails.

Then again, she didn't look like the kind of girl who would eat like Henry VIII either.

Sunshine gave him her usual beaming smile as she reached him. She was wearing a pair of skintight pants in dark green, with a 1960s-style tunic. The tunic was cream, with a psychedelic red and black swirl on the front that should have looked like crap but didn't. She had on the same sun/moon necklace, but no other jewellery. And that was kind of strange too, wasn't it? Where was the bling?

She kissed him on the cheek, same as yesterday, before he could step out of reach, and sat as though exhausted, thumping an oversized tote—rust-coloured canvas—on the floor beside her chair.

'Whew,' she said. 'I've got lots of samples with me, so that bag is heavy.'

Leo couldn't work out how she could wear colours that didn't match—her shoes, her outfits, her bags always seemed to be different shades and tones—and yet everything looked *I'm-not-even-trying* perfect. He'd been out with models and fashion PR types who didn't make it look that easy.

'Did you sort out the guest list with Caleb?' she asked, and had the nerve to twinkle at him.

'Yes,' Leo said unenthusiastically.

'So! A hundred and fifty, right?'

Gritted teeth. 'Yes, a hundred and fifty. But you can still forget every one of the venues you listed as options.' He sounded grumpy, and that made him grumpier—because there was really nothing to be grumpy *about*. It wasn't *his* damned wedding. But it was just...*galling*!

Sunshine observed him, head tilted to one side in her curious bird guise. 'Does that mean you have somewhere fantastic in mind to fit one hundred and fifty people? Somewhere that will be available with only two months' notice?'

'As a matter of fact I do,' Leo said. 'I have a new place opening next month. But it's not in Sydney. It's an hour and a half's drive south. Actually, it's *called* South.'

He was a bit ashamed of himself for sounding so smug about it—what was he? Fifteen years old?—but his smugness went sailing right by Sunshine, who simply clapped her hands, delighted.

Which made him feel like a *complete* churl.

Sunshine Smart was not good for his mental health.

'Oh, I've read about it!' she exclaimed. 'Perched on

the edge of the escarpment, sweeping views of the ocean. Right?'

'Yep.'

Another enthusiastic hand-clap. 'Perfectamundo. When can we go and see it?'

Perfectamundo? Good Lord! 'Not necessary,' he said repressively. 'I've personally handpicked the staff for South, and they know what they're doing. We can just give them instructions and leave them to it. But I can send you photos of the space.'

Sunshine was staring at him as though he'd taken leave of his senses. 'Of course it's necessary. Your staff may be excellent, but Jon is trusting me to make sure everything is perfect. I know exactly what he likes, you see, and I can't let him down.'

Leo sighed inwardly.

'We have to think about how the tables are going to be arranged,' she went on. 'The best place for speeches, where we'll do welcoming cocktails—I mean, is there an outdoor area for that?' Her hands came up, clasped her head at the temples as if she were about to have a meltdown. 'A *thousand* things.'

Leo felt a throb at the base of his skull. 'Let me think about it,' he said, just to staunch the flow of words. He wasn't *really* going to think about taking her to see the damned restaurant.

'Thank you, Leo!' She was back to twinkling, clearly nowhere *near* a meltdown.

Two months! Two *months* of this manipulative, mendacious wretch.

'So!' she said. 'Let's talk invitations. I have three designs to show you—and I won't tell you which is my favourite because I don't want to influence your opinion.'

'You won't.'

'Well, I wonder if, subliminally, knowing what I like

best might sway you.' Little knowing smile. 'Maybe to deliberately pick something that is *not* my favourite! And that would never do.'

He caught his half-laugh before it could surface. Laughing would only encourage her.

'And since we haven't discounted the email, I've got something to show you too,' he put in smoothly, because he'd be damned if his version was going to be dead in the water without a demo at least. 'It's something we did for the Q Brasserie launch.'

Half an hour later Leo was amazed to find that he'd agreed to a printed Art Deco-style invitation in blue and teal, with yellow, brown, and grey accents.

But he'd had a win too! Sunshine was so impressed with his electronic idea she'd insisted they send something like it as a save-the-date notice, linking to some artsy teaser footage of South's surroundings.

'But we'll keep the venue secret,' she added conspiratorially, 'because it will be fun to have everyone guessing, and they'll be so excited to find out it's South when the printed invitations arrive.'

He hoped—he *really* hoped—he hadn't just been soothed.

Sunshine took on the responsibility for getting the invitations printed and addressed, with names handwritten by a calligrapher she'd dated in the past. She would show Leo—who actually didn't give a damn—the final design before it went to print, along with handwriting samples. Leo was in charge of getting the save-the-date done for Sunshine's approval—and she most certainly *did* give a damn.

He was on the verge of disappearing to the kitchen when Sunshine circled back to South and her need to see it.

'It's not going to happen,' Leo said. 'You can't go on site without me. And the only time I have free is…is…daytime Monday.' *Ha!* 'Shop hours for you, right?'

Sunshine pulled out a clunky-looking diary.

He did a double-take. 'You're on Facebook but you use a paper diary?'

'My mother made it for me so I have to—and, anyway, I like it,' she said. 'Hemp and handmade paper. Jon and Caleb have them too. Play your cards right and you'll get one next year. And, yes! I can do Monday. Yay!'

Again with the *yay*. And the twinkle.

And that throb at the base of his skull.

Sunshine put her diary away. 'My hours are super-flexible. I mostly work from home, and usually at night, when I seem to be more creative—not during the day, and never in the shop unless I'm doing a particular display. Because I have a superb manager who would *not* take kindly to my interfering.'

'I like the sound of your manager.'

'Oh, I can introduce— Ah, I see, sarcasm.' She regarded him with a hint of amused exasperation. 'You know, I'm not generally regarded as an interfering person.'

He couldn't keep the snort in.

'Sarcasm and a *snort*! Better not debate that, then. So! Shall I drive us down?'

'I'm going to take my bike.'

Her face went blank. 'Bike?'

'As in motor,' he clarified.

'You have a car as well, though?'

'No, I don't.'

'Because we could get so much done if we drove down the coast together.'

'Except that I don't have a car.'

'But I have a car. You can come with me.'

'Sunshine, I'd better put this out there right now: you are not going to control me. I don't have a car. I have a bike. I am going to ride down the coast, because that is what I want to do. Why don't you just ride down with me?'

Mental slap of his own head! Why the *hell* had he suggested that? Sunshine Smart plastered against his back for an hour and a half? No, thank you!

Although at least she wouldn't be able to talk to him.

Still, she would annoy him just by *being* there. In her skintight pants…full breasts pressed into his back…breathing against the back of his neck…arms around him…hands sliding up under his leather jacket…

What? No. *No!* Why the hell would her hands need to be sliding up there?

'Thanks, but, no,' she said—and it took Leo a moment to realise she was talking about riding on the bike as opposed to sliding her hands under his jacket. *Thanks, but, no.* Sharp and cool—and not open for discussion, apparently.

And it…*stung*! Dammit.

'Why not?' he asked.

'Because I don't like motorbikes.'

Don't like motorbikes! Well, good. Fine. Who cared if Sunshine Smart didn't like motorbikes? Every other woman he dated couldn't *wait* to hop on the back of his Ducati!

Not that he was dating Sunshine Smart. *Argh.* Horrible, horrible thought.

Just let it go. Let it go, Leo.

'Why? Because you can't wear ten-inch heels on one?' That was letting it go, was it?

'I don't wear ten-inch heels anywhere—I'm not a stilt-walker. It's not about shoes. Or clothes. Or even what those helmets do to your hair.' She tossed said hair. 'It's just…' She shrugged one shoulder, looking suddenly uncomfortable. 'Just an antiquated little notion I have about staying alive.'

'Fine,' he snapped. 'You drive, I'll ride, and we'll meet there.'

And then she sort of slumped…without actually slumping. He had an absurd desire to reach over and touch her damned hair, and tell her…what? Tell her *what*?

That he would drive down the coast with her? Hell, no! Not happening. And he was *not* touching her hair. He didn't touch anyone's hair. Ever.

Leo all but leapt to his feet. 'I'd better get into the kitchen.'

'Right now? But—' Sunshine checked her watch. 'Oh. That took longer than I thought.'

She gave her head a tiny shake. Shaking off the non-slumping slump, he guessed, because the perk zoomed back, full-strength.

'I have other samples in my bag—you know, pictures of floral arrangements and cakes. And I was going to talk to you about shoes. I'm arranging some custom-made shoes for you for the big day.'

'Flowers can't be that urgent. I have a superb baker on staff, so don't get carried away on the cake. And I don't need shoes.'

'The shoes are a gift. From me. I'm doing them for Caleb and Jon too. And I promise it will not be an identical shoe gig—nothing like those ancient wedding parties with six groomsmen all wearing pale blue tuxes with dark blue lapel trim!' Dramatic shudder. 'Oh, please say yes, Leo.'

Leo looked down at his feet, at his well-worn brown leather shoes. Scuffed, but as comfortable as wearing a tub of softened butter. And he had other shoes. Good shoes. *Italian* shoes. He didn't need more. He didn't want her goddamned shoes.

But her hypnotically beautiful mismatched eyes were wide and pleading as he looked back up, and he found himself saying instead, 'I'll think about it.'

She smiled. '*Thank* you. There's a ton of stuff still to talk about, but I understand you're on a tight leash tonight, so you get going. And before we meet on Monday I'll do some legwork on the flowers front. And music... No, I won't do any legwork on that, because I know you used to go out with that gorgeous singer Natalie Clarke, and she would be perfect. I hope—' She stopped, bit her lip. 'Oh, dear, enough about the music. I'm sensing a teensy bit of animosity—that little tic next to your mouth gives it away, you know. But we still have clothes to talk about. Yours and mine, since we're the closest thing they'll have to an official wedding party. We don't want to look too matchy-matchy, but there's so much we *can* do to look part of the overall theme.'

Leo stared. He was doing a lot of that. 'You mean there's a *theme*?'

'I'm not talking about those horrifying Elvis or Medieval or Viking themes. Or Halloween—it's been done! I've seen pictures—with pumpkins! I mean just a touch of complementary colour, a certain style...things like that.'

'You're scaring me.'

'I promise you'll love—'

'*Really* scaring me. Later, okay? *Much* later.'

Sunshine wrinkled up her nose—and Leo had now twigged that this meant she was about to put a new argument, so he held up a 'stop' hand.

'I'll see you Monday, Sunshine. And in the meantime try and remember that the marriage will have already happened. This is just a celebratory dinner.'

'But—'

'Monday.'

She made a muted explosive sound, redolent of frustration. 'All right! Monday! But I'm staying here for dinner—not running away like a good little girl.' She tossed her hair again. Flick. Over her shoulder. 'I have a date.'

Leo kind of liked that huffy hair-flick—it made him feel as if *she* were the one off kilter for a change.

'Then I'll send over a Campari for you while you wait.'
Calm. Reasonable. Charming, even.

'Lovely, thank you,' she responded. Calm, reasonable,
charming.

'I won't be able to come out and speak to Gary tonight,
though.'

'That's okay—Gary's not coming.'

Frown. 'But I thought you said...?'

'Oh, I see.' Little laugh. *Annoying* little laugh. 'No, tonight I'm having dinner with Ben.'

'Another investment banker?'

'No. Ben's an embalmer.'

Leo did the stare thing again. 'You're joking, right?'

'No.' Puzzled. Actually, seriously puzzled. 'Why would
that be a joke?'

'An *embalmer*? How did you even get to *meet* an embalmer? Are you making shoes for corpses?'

'Not that I *wouldn't* make shoes for corpses, but no.'
Pause. He saw the tiny swallow. 'It—it was a subject I
needed to—to research. Two years ago. For my...sister.'

'I didn't know you had a sister.' He thought back...
something about her eyes? In the womb... Triplets...?

Twins!

Oh. Embalmer. Sister. Her twin sister was dead. And
he was such a freaking idiot!

Because—oh, God. *no*—the face-morph. It was happening again. Emptiness. Ashy skin. Trembling lips. What
the hell *was* that?

'Sunshine...?'

No response.

'Sunshine!'

Alarmed.

She shook her head and the look was gone. But her eyes
were filling and she was blinking, blinking, blinking, trying to stop the tears falling.

Crap! He reached over to the next table, snagged a napkin, held it out to her with a gruff, 'Here.'

She took the napkin but just stared at it. Another blink.

He watched, holding his breath... Just one tear, one drop, and he would have to...to... No, he couldn't... could he? Hovering, hovering... His heart was starting to pound...

And then she took a long, slow breath and the tears receded.

Leo took his own long, slow breath, feeling as though disaster had just been averted, and slid into the chair beside her.

'Sorry,' Sunshine said. 'My sister died two years ago. The anniversary is coming up so I'm feeling kind of... emotional about it. I should be over it by now, but every now and then...' That tiny head-shake, then she looked at Leo and smiled. 'Anyway, let's get back to—'

'What was her name? Your sister?' Leo asked, because he was not getting back to *anything* quite that easily.

Sunshine paused, but only for a few seconds—and her smile didn't waver at all. 'Are you ready for this, Leo? It's not for the fainthearted.'

Leo didn't know if he was ready, not ready, or why he had to *be* ready.

In fact he didn't know squat.

He didn't know why he hadn't let her change the subject as she'd clearly wanted to do. Why her unwavering smile was bothering him. Why he wanted to take her by the shoulders and shake her until she let those jammed-up tears fall.

He didn't know a damned thing—*least* of all why he should be interested in Sunshine Smart's dead sister.

But he said, 'Worse than Sunshine?'

'Ouch! But, yes—at least Moonbeam thought so.'

'Moonbeam?' He winced. 'Seriously? I mean...*seriously*?'

Little gurgle of laughter. 'Yep.'

'Good God. Moonbeam. And Sunshine.'

She was playing with the hem on the napkin he'd given her, picking at it with her fingernails.

'So what happened?' Leo asked.

She looked down at the napkin. Pick, pick. 'Hippie parents.'

'No, I mean what hap—?'

'Oh, dear, I've snagged the hem,' Sunshine said, and put the napkin on the table. 'Sorry, Leo.'

'I don't care about the napkin, Sunshine.'

'Actually, table napkins have an interesting history. Did you know that they started out as lumps of dough, rolled and kneaded at the table? Which led, in turn, to using sliced bread to wipe your hands.'

What the hell? 'Er—no, I didn't know that.' Thrown. Completely thrown.

Extra-bright smile. 'But you were asking about Moonbeam. Actually, it's because of her that I'm sitting here with you. She and Jonathan dated as teenagers.'

He was staring again—couldn't help it. 'No way!'

'Yes way! But Moon realised pretty quickly that she'd need to swap an X for a Y chromosome if their relationship was going to get to the next level, even though Jon adored her. So—long story short—she encouraged Jon to leap out of the closet, with me hooked in for moral support, and the three of us became super-close—like a *ménage à trois* minus the sex. And *voilà*—here I am, planning Jon's wedding to your brother.' Her brilliant smile slipped. 'One of the reasons I miss Jon so much is because he's a link to my sister.'

Jon dating a girl. *Ménage à trois* minus the sex. Bread as *table napkins*? Leo didn't know what to say.

'Anyway,' she went on, 'I don't have to explain that to you. I know you miss your brother too.'

'It can't compare.'

'Yeah, I guess…I guess you can jump on a plane if you need to see Caleb.'

'That's more likely to happen in reverse.'

'You mean him jumping on a plane? Oh, no, I see— *him* needing to see *you*.' She looked him over. 'I get that. You're the dominant one, you're the one doling out the goods, and you don't *need* to see anyone.'

The perceptiveness startled him.

'So no emotional combustions! It's a good way to be,' she went on. 'In fact my approach to relationships is based on achieving a similar core of aloofness, of control. Of mastery over my emotions.'

He was a little awed. 'Your approach to relationships?'

'Yes. Separating sex from love, for example—you know, like that *ménage à trois* with me, Jon, and Moon. You have to agree that it makes life easier.'

'Easier, maybe. Not better.'

'Of course it's *easiest* to leave the love out altogether. That's what I do now.'

'What? Why?'

She tapped her chest lightly, over her heart. 'No room in here.'

'You're not that type of person.'

'Well, I *do* have to work hard at it,' she conceded.

'What? Why?' God, he was repeating himself!

'Because my natural inclination is to care too much about people. I have to take precautions to guard against that.'

'What? Why?' Nope—he was *not* doing another repeat! 'I mean, what are you scared of?'

'Pain,' she said simply. 'Because it hurts. To care deeply. It hurts.'

Leo wanted to tell her the whole argument was ridiculous, but the words wouldn't come. What did he know? He was living proof that sex was usually loveless, no matter how much you wished otherwise.

At least Sunshine could actually touch a person without having a panic attack, so she was way ahead of him. For sure Gary and Ben wouldn't have let Sunshine have those mini-meltdowns and sat there like blockheads, handing her restaurant napkins. How was he supposed to find what Caleb had when he couldn't put his arms around a tearful woman? Did he even deserve to, stunted as he was?

'But we were talking about embalming,' Sunshine said, and she was twinkling again. 'Which is much more interesting. A very technical and responsible job. And it does make you think, doesn't it?'

Leo, reeling from the various changes in conversation he'd been subjected to for the past few minutes—shoes, pumpkins, napkins, sex, love, embalming, *napkins*—could only repeat stupidly, 'Think…?'

'Well, cremation or burial? It's something we all need to plan for. If you're interested—as you should be, if you ride a motorbike—I'm sure Ben would be happy to—'

'Er, no—that's fine, thanks.' Leo got to his feet with alacrity. 'I'll send over that drink.'

Halfway through the night, Leo poked his head out of the kitchen. Ostensibly to gauge how the place was humming along, but really—he was honest enough to admit it—to check out Sunshine's date.

And Ben the embalmer was handsome enough to give Alexander Skarsgard a run for his money. Like a freaking Viking!

They'd ordered the roast leg of lamb—a sharing dish that came with crispy roast potatoes, crusty bread rolls and assorted side dishes and condiments. Enough food to feed the entire cast of *The Hobbit*, including the trolls.

Twice more Leo peered out at them. Both times Ben

was laughing and Sunshine was about to shove a laden fork in her mouth. Leo was starting to think Sunshine could single-handedly have eating classified as a championship sport.

Since he thought dining with a woman who actually ate would make a nice change, he didn't know why the sight of Sunshine chomping up a storm with Ben was so annoying.

But it was. Very, *very* annoying.

Another laugh floated through the restaurant and into his straining ears.

Right! He ripped off his apron. He was going to find out what the hell was so funny.

He washed his hands, changed into a clean chef's jacket and headed out.

Sunshine looked up, startled. 'Leo! This is a surprise.'

She quickly performed introductions as one of the waiting staff rushed to find a spare chair for Leo, who was examining the almost demolished lamb leg.

Leo raised his eyebrows. 'Didn't like it, huh?' he said, settling into the quickly produced chair.

Sunshine groaned. 'Not funny. I'll have to start dieting tomorrow.'

'That will be a one-day wonder,' Ben said, and winked at Sunshine.

Winked! Who the hell *winked* at people?

Sunshine laughed. 'Or you could kiss me instead, Ben, because—interestingly—kissing burns six and half calories per minute. As long as it's passionate.' She pursed her lips. 'I guess passion supersizes the metabolic effect.'

Ben, in the process of sipping his wine, choked. 'Where do you get all these facts?'

'The internet.'

Ben grinned. 'Better brush up on your arithmetic, Sunny, because if I kiss you for, say, fifteen minutes—and any longer is just *asking* for chapped lips—it's going to net you a hundred calories max. Basically, we'll burn off two thirds of a bread roll.'

'Are you talking yourself out of a kiss?' Sunshine asked.

She was doing the eyelash-bat thing, and Leo decided it made her look like a vacuous twit. He only just stopped himself from telling her so.

Ben smiled at Sunshine. A very *intimate* smile, by Leo's reckoning. 'You know I'm up for it,' he said. 'But we're going to have to make it a marathon and buy a truckload of lip balm if you keep that up.' He nodded at her fingers, which were hovering over the food.

Sunshine snatched up a small piece of crispy potato and popped it into her mouth. 'It's a vegetable,' she said. 'Doesn't count.'

'Oh, that's a *vegetable*!' Ben laughed. 'And you're a *nut*, Sunshine.'

Sunshine smiled serenely. 'If that's the analogy we're going with, you're a piece of meat.'

Ben gave her a *faux* mournful look. 'Oh, I know I'm just a piece of meat to you. We all are.'

A phone trilled.

'Mine,' Ben said, reaching into his shirt pocket. He checked the caller ID. 'Sorry, I have to take this.'

'All?' Leo asked as Ben left the table.

Sunshine laughed. 'Just a "poor me" thing with my exes. They get a bit club-like.'

'What? There's like a *legion* of them?'

Another laugh. 'Not quite.'

Leo leant forward, fixed her with a steady gaze. 'Are you sleeping with both of them? Gary *and* Ben?'

She stopped laughing. 'And you're interested because…?'

'Just wondering where everyone fits in relation to that guff about sex and love you were spouting earlier and the whole pieces of meat thing.'

'It's not guff.'

'*Total* guff.'

She considered him for a moment. 'Well—I've never been in love, but I *have* had sex. And I'll bet you've had enough sex to write *Fifty Shades of Leo*—but no wife. No steady girlfriend, even, right? No…love…perhaps?'

He felt his jaw clamp. God, he'd love to show her fifty shades of Leo. She wouldn't be looking at him in that curious bird way at the end. 'That's not the point,' he ground out.

'That's exactly the point. What's wrong, Leo? Not enough room in there?' She leant over and tapped her fingers on his chest, right over his heart. *Into* his heart, it felt like. 'I don't think you should be lecturing me just because I have sex without love the same as you do.'

'You're supposed to want them both.'

She tossed her head. 'Well, I don't. I won't. Ever. And glowering at me isn't going to change that.'

'I'm not glowering. I don't glower.'

'Oh, you *so* do. It's kind of cute.'

'I'm not cute.'

'Sure you are—in that I'm-a-typical-male-hypocrite kind of way.'

'I'm not a hypocrite either.'

'Go and get yourself nicely monogamised and I'll believe you.'

'Monogamised isn't a real word.'

That twitch at the side of her mouth.

Leo felt his temper surge. 'And I *am* monogamous.'

'Yeah—but one-after-the-other monogamy doesn't count if there's a hundred in the pipeline.'

He wanted to haul her out of her chair and… And what? And *nothing*, that was what. Nothing.

'Ben's coming back so I'll leave you to it,' he said. 'I've got some dessert coming out for you.'

She bit her bottom lip. 'Oh, dear—I really will need to start a diet tomorrow.'

Leo got to his feet. 'Just get Ben to kiss you twice.'

Sunshine grabbed his hand to keep him where he was.

His fingers curled around hers before he could stop them—and then his fingers stiffened. He pulled his hand free, flexed his fingers.

Sunshine's eyes flickered from his hand to his face. There was doubt in her eyes. And concern. And a tenderness that enraged him. He didn't need it. Didn't need Sunshine-bloody-Smart messing with his head or his goddamned hand.

'Why are you upset with me, Leo?' she asked softly.

He was unbearably conscious of the scent of her. Jonquils. A woman who'd just stuffed herself silly with meat shouldn't smell like flowers, so why did she?

'I'm not upset with you,' he said flatly. *Liar.* 'I'll email you a map for Monday.'

He strode back to the kitchen, furious with himself because he *was* upset with her.

But that was the 'what' of the equation. What he couldn't work out was the 'why'.

What? Why?

Oh, for God's sake!

CHAPTER THREE

TO: Jonathan Jones
FROM: Sunshine Smart
SUBJECT: Wedding of the century
Quick update, darling...

Invitations are underway—wording attached. We're going with smart/cocktail as the dress code, although obviously I will be wearing a long dress as befits my bridesmaid status.

Off to check the venue in the morning. It shows every indication of being divine.

Next we'll be working on the menu, but having now eaten at two of Leo's establishments I have no doubt it will be magnificent.

I wish I could meet a chef. Well, obviously I HAVE met one now, but I mean one with jumpable bones!

Sunny xxx

PS—Leo rides a motorbike! And, no, I still haven't done it, but soon.

TO: Caleb Quartermaine
FROM: Leo Quartermaine
SUBJECT: Coming along

Sunshine has the invitations under control and I'm attaching the save-the-date we've decided on. If I don't hear from you in the next day or so I'll go ahead and get this out as per the War and Peace-sized invitation list.

Meeting Sunshine at South in the morning. And if she raises any concerns you'll have to arrange bail for me because I'll kill her.

I'm growing my hair—hope you're happy. And I am apparently having a pair of shoes custom-made for me. Was that your idea? Because I WILL get you back.
LQ

'Wow,' Sunshine said out loud.

South had to have the best position of any restaurant in the whole world.

Well, all right, she hadn't been everywhere in the whole world, and she was sure there must be oodles of well-situated restaurants all over the planet—in fact she would look up 'most scenic restaurants in the world'—but it was spectacular.

The restaurant was perched on the edge of the cliff. But in some mind-blowing engineering feat the entrance to it was positioned actually *over* the cliff and doubled as a small viewing platform. The floor was transparent, so looking down you could see a landscape of trees curving steeply to the beach. Looking directly forward, you could see the deep blue of the ocean; looking to the side and backwards gave you a view into the restaurant. No tables and chairs in there yet, but the space was sharp and clean, with a seemingly endless use of glass to take advantage of the view.

She breathed in the ultra-fresh air. It was windy, and her hair was flying everywhere, but she didn't care. This venue was perfectly…*perfect* for a wedding celebration.

Perfectly perfect. That had been Leo's description of the private room at Q Brasserie. He'd been annoyed with himself over the way he'd described it, which had made her want to hug him, because it was just *not* something to be annoyed about.

Not that he was the cuddly teddy-bear type you could pat and jolly out of the sullens. He was impatient and stand-offish and most of the time just plain monosyllabic cranky. There was no reason at all to feel that he needed to be hugged more often.

And yet…she wanted to put her arms around him right now.

Wanted to be close to him, held by him. Comforting. Comforted.

Dangerous, debilitating thought.

It had to be the proximity of the ocean messing with her head. For which she should have prepared herself before her arrival. Instead here she was, not knowing when or how hard the jolt would hit her—only knowing that it would.

So she would force it—get it done, dealt with, before she saw Leo. She didn't want to slip up in front of him again.

She took a breath in. Out. Looked out and down, focusing her thoughts… And even though she was expecting it to hit, the pain tore her heart. The memory of Moonbeam was so vivid she gasped.

Moonbeam had believed she belonged to the ocean—and Sunshine had always felt invaded, overrun, by the truth of that when she was near the coast, even when she was far above the water, like now.

One of her most poignant memories was of their last time at the beach. Darkness, rain, and Moonbeam exulting as she raced naked into the waves. *'This is where I'm me!'* Moon had yelled, and Sunshine, laughing but alarmed as she tried to coax her out of the freezing, dangerous, roiling surf, had called her a crazy Poseidon-worshipping hippie.

Three days later Moonbeam was dead.

Sunshine touched her sun and moon charms. She longed so keenly for her sister just then she couldn't move, could barely breathe. The loneliness, the hunger to be so close to someone that you were like two sides of the same coin, was like a knife wound. But not a sharp wound; it was a *festering* wound that wouldn't close, wouldn't heal.

'Sunshine?'

She took a moment, forcing the depression to the back of her consciousness with a shake of her head as she'd trained herself to do in public. Defences securely in place, she turned, smiling, to face Leo, who was standing at the doors leading into the restaurant.

'Hi, Leo,' she said.

Leo pushed the heavy doors further open, inviting her to enter. She started to lean up to kiss him as she crossed the threshold, but he jerked away before she could connect and she stumbled. He grabbed her elbow. Released it the nanosecond she regained her balance.

Ah, okay! She got it. He didn't want her to kiss him.

In fact…thinking back over their few meetings…she would go so far as to say he didn't want her to touch him in any way, ever.

And she'd just been daydreaming about putting her arms around him. Way to give the man a heart attack!

Was it just her, or did he have a problem touching all women? And if it was a problem with women generally, how did the man manage to have sex with a human?

Maybe he didn't. Maybe he had a blow-up doll.

Maybe it wasn't just women.

Maybe he had a problem touching men *and* women. Maybe he had a problem touching pets. *And* blow-up dolls.

Maybe he had an obsessive-compulsive disorder, hand-washing thing going on.

Hmm. She'd read something that might help in that case—about systematic desensitisation…or was it exposure therapy…?

In Leo's case it would mean touching him often, to get

him to see that nothing diabolical would happen to him just because of a bit of skin contact.

She could do that.

It would be a public service, almost.

A favour to a man who was going to be family—well, kind of family.

What was more, it would be *fun*.

'Oh, dear. I'm sorry, Leo. I took you by surprise, didn't I?' She bit her lip. 'I should have learned by now not to launch myself at people when they aren't ready! I once ended up in an embarrassing half-kiss, half-handshake, nose-bumping, chokehold situation. Has that ever happened to you?'

'No.'

'Well, just to make sure it never does I'll give you an indicator before I kiss you in future—say…puckering up my lips like a trout, so you'll know it's coming.' She stopped and thought about that. 'Actually, I wonder why they call it a trout pout when women overdo the lip-filler? Trout don't seem to have excessively large lips to me.'

He was looking at her lips now.

'Not that my own lips are artificially inflated, if that's what you're wondering,' she assured him, moving further into the restaurant. 'They're just naturally troutish. If trout really *do* have thick lips, that is. I definitely need to have another look at a photo of a trout.'

Leo's gaze had moved on to her hair. In fact he was looking at it with a moroseness that bordered on the psychotic.

What the *hell* was going on in his head?

'Is something wrong with my hair?' she asked, and flicked a hand at it. 'Do I look like I stuck my finger in an electrical socket? Because it's windy out there.' She reached into her bag—an orange leather tote—and pulled out an elastic band. Bundling the tousled mess of it into a bunch at the back of her head, she tucked the ends under and roughly contained it. 'There—fixed,' she said. 'I need a haircut, but I'm not sure how to style it for the wedding so it has to wait. I have a great hairdresser—actually, I used to date him.'

'*Another* one?'

'Another...? Oh, you mean someone else I used to date? Well, yes. Anyway, Iain—that's my hairdresser—says he needs to see the dress first. Some people might say that's a little neurotic, but he's a genius so I'm not arguing. And, of course, if I did argue it would be a pot-kettle-black thing, because I'm just as neurotic. I can't design your shoes, for example, until I know what you're wearing.'

He looked a heartbeat away from one of those glowers he supposedly didn't do. It was his only response.

'That was a hint, by the way, to let me know what you're wearing.'

'Yep, I got that.'

Silence.

'So!' she said. 'What do you think? About my hair? Should I keep the fringe? It won't grow out completely in two months, but it should be long enough to style differently—say, like...' She pushed the fringe to one side, smoothing it across her temple.

'I like the fringe,' Leo said.

Words! Yay! But he was *still* frowning.

And now he was looking at her dress.

Okay, so it was a little tight—hello! After two nights in a row at his restaurants, never mind yesterday's two-minute noodles, sugar donuts, and family block of chocolate, what did he expect? But nothing *that* remarkable. Kind of conservative. Just a nude-coloured woollen sheath. V-neck, knee-length, three-quarter sleeves, no fussy trim.

His eyes kept going, down her legs to her shoes. Five-inch-high nude pumps.

'Problem?' she asked, when his eyes started travelling back up, and she must have sounded exasperated because that stopped him.

At last he looked in her eyes. 'You look good—as usual.'

Oh. 'Thank you,' she said, and actually felt like preening.

'But I don't want you to break your neck wriggling around in that dress and tottering on those heels. The building is finished but there's still some debris around that you could trip over.'

And we're back!

This was going to be a long day. A long, *fun* day. He was just so irresistibly grumpy!

She stepped towards the windows. 'This is just brilliant!' Turned to shoot him a broad smile. 'Are you going to give me a tour, Leo?'

He nodded—and looked so uninviting that Sunshine almost laughed. Well, there was no time like the present to commence his therapy and start touch, touch, touching!

Brace yourself, Leo darling.

'Yes, but be careful,' Leo was saying, oblivious. 'And leave your bag—it looks heavy.'

Sunshine dropped the bag on the spot. 'Tell you what,' she said, walking back to him, 'I'm just going to hold on to you so you don't have to worry about the state of my fragile limbs.' She took his arm before he could back away. His arm felt hard and unyielding, like a piece of marble. Or petrified wood. Petrified! Perfect. She beamed up at him. 'Lead on, Leo.'

His jaw was shut so tightly she thought he might crack a tooth.

Oh, dear...oh, deary me! This was going to be *good.*

This was *bad,* Leo realised.

Actually, he'd realised it the moment he saw her standing on the viewing platform outside, looking glamorous and yet earthy. And wistful. And…sad.

So she was sad—so what? She recovered like lightning, didn't she? Like the other times. There was no reason for him to want to… Well, no reason for anything.

And her hair was annoying! Out on the platform the wind had been blowing it every which way and she hadn't given a thought to the tangle it was creating, and then she'd shoved the mess of it into a band as though it didn't matter. She *should* care about her damned hair the way every other woman he'd ever dated cared.

Not that he was dating her.

It was destabilising, that was all, to have his perceptions mucked around with.

As was the way she'd cast that expensive-looking orange leather carry-all thing onto the floor—as though it were no more valuable than a paper shopping bag.

And the fact that she never wore nail polish.

The way she could make her eyes twinkle at will.

And that fresh flower smell of hers.

The jolt when she took his arm and looked up at him with mischief printed all over her face like a tattoo.

He didn't want to feel gauche when he pulled away from her touch and nearly caused her to face-plant—and then embarrassed because she laughed it off and blamed herself when he *knew* that *she* knew the fault was his. Because Sunshine, he was coming to realise, was no dummy.

And he certainly didn't want to feel disapproving, like a damned priest, just because she was dating two men simultaneously and didn't love either of them. Because she was right about one thing: who was he to lecture her?

Leo flexed his arm under her hand, which felt disturbingly light and warm and…whatever. It was nothing. Meant nothing. It was just her keeping her balance. The same as holding on to a railing.

He took a slow, silent breath. 'Let's start with the kitchen,' he said, and led her though swinging doors into a large room of gleaming white tiles and spotless stainless steel surfaces. 'Everything in here is state of the art, from the appliances to the ventilation system.'

Sunshine let go of his arm—relief!—and turned a slow circle. 'It's kind of daunting. Although I think that about every kitchen.'

'You don't like to cook?'

'I just do *not* cook. I can't. I did once boil an egg, although it ended up hard like the inside of a golf ball.' That stopped her for a moment. Distracted her. 'Have you ever peeled off the outer layer of a golf ball?' she asked. 'It's amazing inside—like an endless rubber band wrapped round and round.'

Not exactly a riveting fact, but she did seem to have an interest in the oddest subjects. 'You boiled it too long,' he said. *Yeah, I kind of think she figured that out herself, genius.*

'I ate it, but I haven't boiled an egg since. And, really, why boil an egg when you can pop out to a café and have one perfectly poached with some sourdough toast?'

'And that's the only thing you've cooked? The egg?'

'I've made two-minute noodles—as recently as yesterday.'

'Didn't you help out at home when you were a kid?'

'That was the problem.' She ran a finger along the pristine edge of one of the cooker tops. 'My hippie parents are vegetarian. It was all bean sprouts, brown rice and tofu—which I actively detest—when I was growing up.' She gave one of those exaggerated shudders that she seemed to luxuriate in. 'Tofu casserole! Who wants to cook *that*?'

She opened an oven, peeked inside.

'You're clearly a *lapsed* vegetarian.'

She turned to face him. 'Capital L, lapsed! From the

moment I bit into a piece of sirloin at the age of fifteen—on a Wednesday, at seven-thirty-eight p.m.—I was a goner. I embraced my inner carnivore with a vengeance. Meat and livestock shares skyrocketed! And two days later I tried coconut ice and life was never the same again. Hello, processed sugar! I don't have *a* sweet tooth—I have a shark's mouth full of them!'

'Shark's mouth?'

'Specifically, a white pointer. Did you know they have something like three hundred and fifty teeth? Fifty teeth in the front row and seven rows of teeth behind, ready to step up to the plate if one drops out.'

This was more interesting than the make-up of a golf ball, but not quite as intriguing as the calorific benefit of a passionate kiss.

And he wished he hadn't remembered that kiss thing—because it came with a vision of her kissing the Viking embalmer.

Sharks. Think about sharks. 'The only thing I know about sharks' teeth is that they can kill you,' he said.

'Hmm, yes, although the chance is remote. Like one in two hundred and fifty million or something. You've got more chance of being killed by bees, or lightning, or even fireworks! But that was just an illustrative example. So! I'm a processed-sugar-craving carnivore, to my parents' chagrin.' She stopped. Took a breath. 'Seriously, I must have the metabolism of a hummingbird, because otherwise I'd be in sumo wrestler territory. You know, hummingbirds can eat three times their own weight every day!' She ran a hand down her side and across her belly. 'Not that I can do *that*, of course,' she said sadly.

'No,' Leo agreed. 'You're not exactly skinny.'

A surprised laugh erupted from her. 'Thank you, Leo. Music to every girl's ears!'

'That wasn't an insult. I'm a chef—I like to see people eating.'

'In that case, stick with me and you'll be in a permanent state of ecstasy.'

And there it was—*wham!*—in his head. The image of her licking the glaceé off her spoon. Ecstasy.

He swallowed—hard. 'You could take a cooking class.'

'I think the cooking gene was bored out of me by the time I left the commune.'

'The commune? So not only are your parents hippies but you lived on a *commune*?'

'And it was *not* cool, if that's what you're thinking. Less of the free love, dope-smoking and contemplating our navels, and more of the sharing of space and chores and vehicles. Scream-inducing. If you have any desire for even a modicum of privacy do *not* join a commune.' She did the twinkle thing. 'And, really, *way* too much hemp clothing. Not that I have anything against hemp—I mean, did you know the hemp industry is about ten thousand years old? Well, probably you didn't know and don't care. But you have to admit that's remarkable.' Stop. Breathe. 'However, let's just say that I don't want to wear it every day.'

Oddly enough, Leo could see her wearing hemp. On weekends, down at the edge of the surf, with her hair blowing all over her face and her polish-free toes in the water.

It must have been the mention of the commune, because that was not a good-time girl Sunshine Smart image.

Enough already! 'Let's move on,' Leo said.

'What about plates, cutlery, glasses, serving dishes? You're sure everything will be here in time?'

'Yes, it will all be here. And it is all brand-new, top-quality, custom-designed.'

'Not that I have any intention of telling you how to stock your restaurant…' She bit her lip. 'But can you send me photos?'

Leo sighed heavily. 'Yes, I can send you photos.'

'Excellent. And can I see the bathrooms?'

She took his arm again, and he didn't quite control a flinch. Thankfully Sunshine seemed oblivious, although he was starting to believe she was oblivious to approximately nothing.

Escorting her into the men's and women's restrooms as though they were out for an arm-in-arm stroll along the Champs-Elysées felt surreal, but Leo knew better than to argue. He wouldn't put it past her to start imparting strange-but-true facts about the toilet habits of some ancient African tribe if he did, and his nerves couldn't take it.

At least she looked suitably dazzled by what she found. Ocean-view glass walls on the escarpment side, with the other walls painted in shifting shades of dreamy blue. Floors that were works of art: murals made of tiny mosaic tiles, depicting waves along the coast. And everything else stark white.

'I could live in here—it's so beautiful!' Sunshine marvelled.

'And I will, of course, send you a photo of the toilet paper we're using,' Leo deadpanned as they walked back to the dining area.

Sunshine looked at him, struck, lips pursing. Leo could almost see the cogs turning.

'You know,' she said slowly, 'I read something somewhere about a pop star who has *red* toilet paper provided when she's on tour, so do you think—?'

'No, I do not,' he interrupted. 'Forget the red toilet paper.'

The nose was wrinkling. 'Well obviously not *red*. I was going to suggest a beautiful ocean-blue. Or sea-green.'

'No blue. Or green. You'll have to content yourself with your victory over my growing hair.'

Sunshine laughed, giving up. 'It's coming along very nicely.'

She ran her hand over the stubble on his head and his whole body went rigid.

Leo stepped away from her, forcing that hand to drop and simultaneously dislodging her other hand from his arm. 'And so are your eyes,' he said, just for something to say—and didn't *that* sound bloody fatuous? How could eyes *come along*? They were just there—from birth!

Although…hmm…something about them wasn't right. Her pupils were a little bigger than they should be, given all the light streaming into the room.

Why were they standing so close that he could see her damned pupils anyway? It wasn't a crowded nightclub. They were the only two people in a big, furniture-free space. There was nothing to bump into. No reason for them to occupy the same square foot of floor. He took another step back from her.

She was considering him with a blinking, slightly dazed look that worried him on a level he didn't want to acknowledge.

And there went that tic beside his mouth.

'I saw my parents yesterday,' she said, and her voice sounded kind of…breathy. 'They like the new natural look—as you could imagine. Mum talked about sending you a thank-you card, so brace yourself for some home-made paper and a haiku poem. Apologies in advance for the haiku!' Stop. Little laugh. 'But strangers are doing a double-take when they look at my eyes now, which makes me feel a bit naked.'

'Don't knock naked. I've had some of my best moments naked,' Leo said, and wondered what the hell was happening to his brain. Disordered. That was what it was. You didn't go from talking about hair to eyes to nakedness. At least *he* didn't.

In fact there was altogether too much talk of underwear, orgasms and sex between them as it was, without tossing *naked* around.

He took yet another step back. Tried to think of something to say about homemade paper instead, because he sure knew nothing about haiku poetry. But Sunshine was giving him that dazed, blinking look, and he couldn't seem to form a word.

'Yeah, me too,' she said.

Leo had a sudden vision of Sunshine naked, lying on his bed. The almost translucent white skin, the long chocolate hair. Voluptuous. Luscious. Steamy hot. Smiling at him, sea-eyes sparkling.

He shook his head, trying to get the image out of his head.

And then Sunshine shook *her* head. 'So! Tables!' she said, and took hold of his arm again—and this time it seemed to hit him straight in the groin.

Leo, looking everywhere *except* at Sunshine, had never enthused so happily about inanimate objects in his life. The choice of wood for the chairs; the elegant curved backs; the crisp white tablecloths and napkins; the bar's marble top and designer stools. And still his bloody erection would not go down!

Go down. Sunshine Smart going down. On him.

Bad.

This was bad, bad, bad.

Walking a little stiffly, he showed her the outdoor terrace. Talked about welcome cocktails. Described the way the decking had been stained to match the wooden floor inside. Back in. Suggested positions for the official table. Indicated places for dancing—except that Caleb had told him that dancing was likely to be off the agenda, so why he was pointing that out was a mystery. Just filling the space with words. *Any* words. Waiting for that erection to subside.

And at the end, when she looked at him with those

twinkling blue and green eyes of hers, he still had a hard-on and he could still—*dammit!*—imagine her naked. On his bed. Kneeling in front of him. Walking towards him. Away from him.

Help!

'Can you email me the layout so I can refresh my memory when I need to?' Sunshine asked. 'Oh—and tomorrow I'll have the invitation design to sign off. Are you happy for me to do it, or would you like to see it?'

'I'd like to see it,' he said, and couldn't believe he'd actually said that. Because He. Did. Not. Care.

'I could email it.'

'No. Not email.'

Sunshine pursed her lips. Her 'thinking' look—not that he knew how he knew that.

'I really do have to be in the store tomorrow,' she said. 'Some new stock is coming in and I have a very specific idea for the display. And you're working tomorrow night, right?'

'No—night off,' he said, and was amazed again. He *never* took a night off.

She brightened. 'Great. Where shall we meet?'

'I'll cook.' Okay. He had lost his mind. He was *not* going to cook for Sunshine Smart. He never cooked for girlfriends. And she wasn't even that. Not even *close* to that. Even if he did want to have sex with her.

Damn, damn, damn. Goddamn.

Sunshine's eyes had lit up like a Christmas tree. 'Really?'

Could he back out? Could he? 'Um. Yes.'

'At my place?'

No—not at her place. Not anywhere. 'Um. Yes.' So he had a vocabulary problem today. Brain-dead. He was brain-dead.

'Just one teensy problem. Most of my kitchen appliances have never been used.'

'I love virgin appliances.' *Arrrgggghhh.* Again with the sexual innuendo. He was clearly on the verge of a nervous breakdown.

'In that case you will have an orgasm when you walk in my kitchen.'

Orgasms. Oh. My. *God.*

Sunshine checked her watch. 'And, speaking of orgasms, I'd better go.'

Huh? What the hell*?*

'I'm being taken to that new Laotian restaurant the Peppercorn Tree tonight,' she said, as though that explained anything. 'I checked the menu online. *Very* excited!'

Okay, he got it. *Whew.* It was the thought of *food* making her orgasmic.

And then her words registered. 'Being taken'. As in date.

'Gary or Ben?' He just couldn't seem to stop himself from asking.

'Neither of them. Tonight it's Marco.'

Marco. *Marco*? *Three* men on a string now? Not to mention the calligrapher. And the hairdresser. And there was probably a butcher, a baker, and a candlestick-maker in there somewhere.

'You sure there was no free love on that commune?' he asked, and thanked heaven and hell that he sounded his normal curt self.

'Love's never free, is it?' Sunshine asked cryptically. And then she smiled. 'That's why I'm only interested in sex.'

Before Leo could think of a response she tap-tapped her way out of the restaurant, clearly with no idea he was having a conniption and might need either medical or psychiatric intervention.

CHAPTER FOUR

TO: Sunshine Smart
FROM: Leo Quartermaine
SUBJECT: Photos
Attached are the images we discussed yesterday, plus the restaurant layout with a sketchy floor plan.

I've also included a photo of the toilet paper. White.

I'll be making pasta tonight, and bringing some home-made gelato.

LQ

TO: Jonathan Jones
FROM: Sunshine Smart
SUBJECT: All going swimmingly—and shoes!
Darling!

Checked out the venue yesterday—scrumptious. Caleb has photos.

Your shoe design is attached. As requested, not too over the top! Black patent with a gorgeous charcoal toe-cap. The shoes will work brilliantly with the dark grey suit and red tie.

I'm sending Caleb's design to him directly—he says you don't get to see his outfit before the big day! And you have the contact number for Bazz in Brooklyn to get the shoes made, so make an appointment, and quickly because he's super-busy.

Leo's are next. And, speaking of Leo...drumroll... tonight he's cooking me dinner!

We'll get onto the wedding menu tonight too. I'm thinking we should lean towards seafood, but with a chicken alternative for those who are allergic, and, of course, a vegetarian (dullsville) option.

Sunny xxx

PS: Was Marco Valetta always such a douche? Had dinner with him last night and he spent the whole meal talking about his inheritance—scared his father is going to gobble it up on overseas travel. Seriously, let the man spend his own money any way he wants! Marco thought he was going to get lucky, but after banging on all night about money and then suddenly switching to the subject of lap dances??????? As if!!!! He is SO off my Christmas card list. I'll bet Leo Quartermaine would never be such a loser.

PPS: I saw a statistic recently that said about twenty-five million dollars is spent on lap dances each year in Vegas alone. Amazing!!!!

TO: Leo Quartermaine
FROM: Caleb Quartermaine
SUBJECT: Loving the Sunshine...

...and I don't mean the New York weather, which is icky-sticky right now.

Just warning you, bro, that my custom-designed shoes are eye-poppers. I love them—but I'm the flamboyant type. Better prepare yourself!

Love the invitations, love the save-the-date, love the fact that you sent Sunshine a photo of the restaurant toilet rolls (yep, she told me). Think I love Sunshine too if she can get you to do that. Jon tells me half the male population of Sydney is in love with her—gay and straight—so I'm in good company.

Also glad about your hair—go, Sunshine! And glad about South.

Can't wait to marry Jon. Seriously, I don't care where or how we do it, as long as we do it. The party is just the icing on an already delicious cake.

Your turn now. Hope you're out there hunting instead of spending every spare minute slaving over assorted hot stoves.

And please tell me the bunny-boiler Natalie is under control. If she turns up at the reception I am getting out the power tools and going for her.

CQ

SUNSHINE LIVED IN an apartment in Surry Hills. The perfect place for people who didn't cook, because wherever you looked there were restaurants. Every price range, every style, and practically every ethnicity.

Leo had sent a ton of supplies and equipment ahead of him, because he had a shrewd understanding of what he could expect to find in Sunshine's cupboards—i.e., nothing much—and the thought of overbalancing the bike while lugging a set of knives was a little too Russian roulette for his liking.

He'd been cursing himself all day about offering to cook for her. Cursing some more that he'd offered to do it at her apartment—his own, with a designer kitchen and every appliance known to man, would have been so much easier. But then, of course, he wouldn't get to see what her place was like. And, all right, he admitted it: he was curious about that. He imagined boldly coloured walls, exotic furniture, vibrant rugs, maybe some kick-ass paintings or a centrepiece sculpture.

He buzzed the apartment and she answered quickly.
'Leo!'
He could hear the excitement in her voice. How did she

do that? Could she really, truly, be that enthusiastic about everything?

'Yep.'

'Fourth floor,' she said, and clicked open the door to the lobby.

She was waiting for him, apartment door wide open, when he got out of the lift.

Her hair was piled on top of her head—kind of messy, but very sexy. She was wearing an ankle-length red kaftan in some silky material that managed to both cling and flow. It had a deep V neckline and was gathered at the base of her sternum behind a fist-sized disc of matching beads. Voluminous sleeves were caught tightly at the wrists. She looked like a cross between a demented crystal healer and a Cossack dancer—but somehow bloody amazing.

His eyes, inevitably, dropped to her feet. She was barefoot. *Good God! Stop the presses.*

'I am *so* looking forward to this,' Sunshine confided, and puckered her lips.

Leo steeled himself, and after the tiniest hesitation she went right ahead and laid the kiss on him.

'That pucker was enough warning, right?' she asked with a cheeky smile. And then she rolled right on before he could answer. 'And I was right—trout do *not* have especially thick lips. So! This way,' she threw over her shoulder, and walked to the kitchen.

She gestured to three boxes on the counter. 'Your stuff arrived about ten minutes ago.'

'Good. I'll unpack everything,' he said, but he was more interested in the uninterrupted view into her apartment afforded by the open-plan kitchen.

And it was…disappointing.

White walls. No paintings. A serviceable four-seater dining suite in one section of a combined living/dining room in a nondescript, pale wood—pine, maybe. The couch was basic, taupe-coloured. A low coffee table in front of the couch matched the dining suite. There was a television atop a cabinet that matched the other furniture. Carpet a similar shade to the couch. Absolutely nothing wrong with any of it, but…no. Just *no*!

He nodded towards the living room. 'What's with the porridge-meets-oatmeal thing out there?' he asked, shrugging out of his leather jacket, and tossing it onto one of the stools on the other side of the kitchen counter.

'Oh, I thought you'd like it.'

Leo was speechless for a moment. Seriously? *That* was how she saw him?

When she came to his apartment she would see just how wrong she was!

Not that she *would* be coming to his apartment. But if she *did*…

Nope, he had to address this now or he wouldn't be able to cook. 'You've seen my restaurants—do they look like they've been furnished from a Design for Dummies catalogue?'

'I guess I didn't imagine you did that part personally. But there's nothing intrinsically wrong with a neutral colour palette, you know! And… Well…' She waved a hand at the living area. 'This part wasn't me, or it would be very different.'

'So who was it?'

'Moonbeam—and she just went for quick, basic, affordable. Out here and in her own room.'

'But aren't twins supposed to…you know…have the same taste?'

'Negativo.'

'So that's a no, is it?' Leo asked dryly.

'A big no way, José.'

Eye-roll. 'So, no?'

'Okay! No.' Matching eye-roll. And then she smiled softly. 'Unlike me, Moon didn't care about *stuff*.'

'What did she care about?'

'Life, the earth, the universe…et cetera.'

'So it stands to reason she wouldn't expect you to make a shrine out of a few pieces of pine, right? Why don't you change it?'

'I can't.'

'Why not?'

'I just…can't.' She looked at the boring furniture as though it were some Elysian landscape. 'Don't you ever want to freeze a moment? Just…*freeze* it? Hang on to it?'

'No, Sunshine, never,' he said. 'I want to move on. And on and on.'

She turned to him. 'You're lucky to be able to see things that way.'

'Actually, it's the *absence* of luck that made me see things that way. The desire to *change* my luck. To have more—a better life. To get…everything.'

Their eyes caught…held.

And then Sunshine gave that tiny shake of the head. 'Anyway,' she said, 'there's quite enough me in this apartment. I just keep it behind closed doors because it's scary for the uninitiated.'

Was she talking about her bedroom? 'Closed doors?'

She pointed at a closed door at one end of the living area. 'My office.' Pointed at another closed door behind her. 'Bedroom.'

Leo's mouth had gone dry. Over a freaking *room*? No—over just the *thought* of a room! But he couldn't help it. 'Show me,' he said.

She twinkled at him. 'You're not ready for that, Leo. But think a cross between Regency England and the Mad Hatter's tea party in the office, and Scheherazade meets Marie Antoinette in the bedroom…'

He looked at the bedroom door hard enough to disgust himself. What did he think was going to happen? An 'Open Sesame' reveal? Why did he care anyway?

'So! Leo! How do we start this gastronomic enterprise?'

Leo dragged his Superman-worthy gaze away from the bedroom door and refocused on Sunshine—the vivid, unique, laughing eyes; the luxuriant hair; her free-spirited yet glamorous dress; her naked feet.

'You're not wearing any shoes,' he said. *Duh! Of course she knows she isn't wearing shoes! They're her feet, aren't they?*

'I'm generally barefoot when I'm at home. But I do have a lovely pair of black beaded high heels that I wear with this dress if I'm going out.'

He could picture her, tap-tapping her way into South with sparkles on her feet, the red silk billowing. He knew he was staring at her feet, but they were very sexy feet.

And then his eyes travelled up. Up, up, up… To find her watching him, her eyes dazed and wide, lips slightly parted.

She licked her lips.

'Sunshine…' he said.

'Yes?' It was more a breath than a word.

'Um…' What? What was he doing? *What?* 'Feet.' *Doh!* 'I mean shoes!' he said desperately. 'I mean mine.'

She looked down at his feet. 'I like them. Blue nubuk. Rounded, desert boot-style toe. White sole.' Her eyes were travelling up now, as his had done. 'Perfect with…'

Holy freaking hell. He hoped she couldn't see his erection as she got to—

Argh. He saw the swallow, the blink, the blush. She'd seen it.

'Jeans,' she finished faintly.

Disaster. This was a freaking disaster. *Say something,*

say something, say something. 'I meant for…for the…the wedding,' Leo said.

And, really, it was a valid subject. Because he was starting to get curious about what she would design for him. Although it would probably end up being the shoe equivalent of a Design for Dummies pine bookshelf: plain black leather lace-ups.

'Oh!' She took a breath, smoothed the front of her dress. 'Well! I need to see what you're wearing first, remember?' She blinked, smiled a little uncertainly. 'So! Pasta? I even bought an apron!'

Food. Good. Excellent. Something he could talk about without sounding stupid or crotchety or boring or…or crazed with inappropriate lust.

Because he could *not* be in lust with Sunshine Smart. They were polar opposites in every single possible, conceivable way. Like light and dark. Bright and gloomy. Joyful and… *Oh, for God's sake, get over yourself!*

'You've got pots and pans, right?' he asked.

'Yes. And most of them are even unpacked.'

'*Most* of them? How long have you lived here?'

'Two and a half years.'

Leo ran his hand over his head. If he'd had hair he would have yanked it. Two and a half years was long enough to unpack *all* the pots and pans. 'I need a medium saucepan and a large frying pan. And what about bowls? Plates? Cutlery?'

'Oh, plates and stuff I have.'

'You get all that out while I unpack the food.'

She started humming. Off-key.

Leo peeked as she opened cupboards and slid out drawers. Just the bare minimum.

He opened the fridge to stow the wine he'd brought— empty except for butter, milk, soda water, and a wedge of Camembert.

Freezer: a bottle of vodka and half a loaf of bread.

The kitchen had one of those slide-out pantry contraptions, which he opened with trepidation. A jar of peanut butter. A packet of lemon tea. A box of sugary kids' cereal. A tin of baked beans that looked a thousand years old. And—sigh—three packets of two-minute noodles.

'Right,' she said proudly, and pointed to the pot, pan, bowls, and forks she had lined up on the counter. She reminded him of a hyperactive kitten being given a ball of wool to play with after being cooped up with nothing all day.

'How old are you?' he asked suddenly.

'Twenty-five—why?'

'You look younger. You act younger.'

'So I'm fat *and* immature?'

'You're not fat.'

She laughed. 'But I *am* immature? Just because I can't cook pasta? How unfair. I'm not asking you to design a boot, am I?'

'Yeah, yeah. Just go and put on your apron,' he said, and then wondered what he thought he was doing as she hurried towards a tiny alcove off the kitchen. What *she* thought she was doing! She wasn't going to be in the kitchen with him! She didn't cook! She had scoffed at the idea of cooking classes. So she didn't need a goddamned apron.

But when she came back she was beaming, and he couldn't find the will to tell her to go and watch TV while he made dinner.

He took one look at the slogan on the front of her apron— *Classy, Sassy, and a Bit Smart-Assy*—and had to bite the inside of his cheek to stop the smile. He was *not* going to be charmed. Like Gary and Ben—and probably Marco. Iain. And the tinker, the tailor, the soldier, and the spy.

'Come on, it's cute—admit it!' she said, possibly wondering about the strangled look on his face. 'You know, I used to be called Sunshine Smart-Ass in school, so see-ing this in the shop today was like an omen. Not a creepy Damien omen. I mean like a sign that I am going to nail this pasta thing.'

'Smart-Ass. Why am I not surprised?' Leo asked through his slightly twisted mouth. Damn, he wanted to laugh.

She'd messed up her hair, getting the apron on. He could see part of her temple, where her fringe had been pushed aside. He realised he was holding his breath. Because... because he wanted to kiss her there.

Half the male population of Sydney is in love with her, he reminded himself. *And you are not—repeat* not—*going to become a piece of meat in the boyfriend brigade.*

Leo unpacked his knives and chopping boards, liberated extra plates and dishes from the cupboard, unearthed ad-ditional gadgets from his magic boxes.

'Come here so you can see properly,' he said as he started arranging ingredients on the counter.

Sunshine moved enthusiastically to stand beside him. The wave of heat emanating from him was very alluring. She edged a little closer. Breathed in the scent of him, which was just...well, just *him*. Just super-clean Leo. Could she manage to get just a bit closer, so that she was just—*nearly*—touching him, without him panicking and hitting her with a cooking implement?

His arm, naked below the short sleeve of his T-shirt, brushed hers—*that* was how close she was, because there was no way he would have done that on purpose—and she felt like swooning. Wished, quite passionately, that she hadn't worn sleeves so she could feel him skin to skin.

And it had absolutely *nothing* to do with exposure ther-apy either.

It was, plain and simple, about sexual attraction. *Mu-*

tual sexual attraction—at least she hoped the impressive bulge in his jeans that had taken her by surprise earlier was Sunshine-induced and not some erectile dysfunction... like that condition called priapism she'd read about on the internet...

Not that she was going to ask him that, of course, because men could be sensitive.

But with or without erectile dysfunction, she wanted to have sex with Leo Quartermaine!

Was it because he was cooking for her? There was definitely something off-the-chain seductive about a man—a *chef* man—making her dinner.

But...no. It was more than that.

Something that had been sneaking up on her.

Something to do with the way he jumped a foot inside his skin when she kissed him on the cheek. The little tic at the corner of his mouth that came and went, depending on his level of agitation. The slightly fascinated way he looked at her, as though he couldn't believe his eyes. And listened to her as though he couldn't believe his ears. The way he gave in a lot, but not always. And how, even when he let her have her way, the *way* he did it told her he might not always be so inclined, so she was not to take it for granted.

How bizarre was that? She liked that he gave in—and also that maybe he wouldn't!

She even kind of liked the fact that he tried so hard never to smile or laugh—as though that would be too frivolous for the likes of him. It was a challenge, that. Something to change. Because everyone needed to laugh. The average person laughed thirteen times a day. She would bet her brand-new forest-green leaf-cut stilettoes that Leo Quartermaine didn't get to thirteen even in a whole year! Not good enough.

Now that she'd acknowledged the attraction it felt moth-to-a-flame mesmeric, standing beside him. No, not a moth—that was too fluttery. More like the bat that had flown smack into the power line a block from her apartment. She'd seen it this morning, fried into rigidity, felled by a jolt of electricity.

Poor bat. Just going along, thinking it had everything under control, contemplating its regular upside-down hang for the night, then hitting a force that was greater than it and—*frzzzzz*. All over, red rover.

Poor bat—and poor her if she let herself get too close to Leo. Because she had a feeling he could fry her to a crisp if she let him.

Not that she would let him. She *never* got too close. That was the whole point of her 'four goes and goodbye' rule. Protecting her core.

Leo had managed to move a little away from her—which she rectified.

'This is a simple fettuccine with zucchini, feta, and prosciutto,' he said, clueless.

He moved once more, just a smidgeon. And Sunshine readjusted her position so she was just as close as before. *Poor Leo—you really should just give up!*

He managed another little edge away. 'We're going to fry some garlic, grated zucchini, and lemon zest, and then toss that through the pasta with some parsley, mint, and butter. Finally we'll throw in some feta and prosciutto—again tossed through—with a little lemon juice, salt, and pepper.'

He was—gamely, Sunshine thought—ignoring the fact that she was practically breathing down his neck.

He cleared his throat. Twice. 'This—' he was showing her a container '—is fresh pasta from Q Brasserie. I thought about making it here, but that might have been too much for a two-minute noodler to cope with.' He shot her a teeny-tiny smile—more of a glint than a smile, but *wowee*! *Be still my heart, or what?*

Sunshine watched as Leo started grating the zucchini

with easy, practised efficiency. There was a long scar on his left thumb, and what looked like a healed burn mark close to his right wristbone. Assorted other war wounds. These were not wimpy hands.

And, God, she wanted his sure, capable, scarred hands on her. All over her. It was almost suffocating how much she wanted that.

She kept watching, a little entranced, as Leo set the zucchini to one side, then grated the lemon rind. Next he grabbed some herbs and started tearing with his beautiful strong fingers as he talked…

His voice was deep and kind of gravelly. '…into strips,' Leo said.

Hmm… She had no idea what the start of that sentence had been.

He unwrapped a flat parcel—inside were paper-thin slices of prosciutto—and put it in front of her. 'Okay?' he asked.

'Sure,' she said, figuring out that she was supposed to chop it, and grabbed a knife.

'No,' Leo said, and took the knife away.

Lordy, Lordy. He'd actually touched her.

Sunshine felt every one of the hairs on her arm prickle. She was staring at him. She knew she was.

He was staring back.

And then he stepped back, cleared his throat again. 'Tear—like this,' he said, and demonstrated. Another clear of the throat. 'You do that and I'll…I'll…find the …cheese.'

She was humming again as she massacred the prosciutto.

And blow him down if it wasn't a woeful attempt at Natalie's signature song—the truly hideous '*Je t'aime-ich liebe-ti amor You Darling*'.

He started crushing garlic with the flat of his knife as though his life depended on it.

She was still tearing. And humming. *Please* tell him she didn't have the same insane cheesy love song obsession as Natalie. Who was *not* going to be performing at his brother's wedding! Once when he'd been mid-thrust, and Natalie had sung a line of that awful song, he'd choked so hard on a laugh he'd given himself a nosebleed; that evening had *not* ended well.

'Done,' Sunshine said, and looked proudly at the ripped meat in front of her.

Leo winced.

'What do you want me to do next?' she asked, with that damned glow that seemed to emanate from her pores.

'Salad,' he said, sounding as if he'd just announced a massacre.

Which it was likely to be—of the vegetable kind.

'We'll keep it simple,' he said. 'Give these lettuce leaves a wash.'

Sunshine took the lettuce leaves and ran them under the tap, her glow dimming.

'What's wrong?' he asked as he took them from her.

'Salad. It's so…vegetarian.'

She looked so disgruntled Leo found himself wanting to laugh again. He swallowed it. 'It's just a side dish. And there's meat in the pasta, remember?'

She wrinkled her nose. *Oh-oh.* Convoluted argument coming.

'I'll do it with a twist,' he offered quickly. 'I'll put some salmon in it, and do a really awesome dressing that doesn't taste remotely healthy. All right?'

Her nose unwrinkled. 'Okay, *if* you go a little heavy on the salmon and a little light on the lettuce.'

He choked. 'Am I designing that boot for you? No? Then

just shut up and see if you can cut these grape tomatoes into quarters. They're small, so be careful.'

She mumbled something derogatory about tomatoes, but made a swipe with the knife.

'Quarter—not slice,' Leo put in.

She nodded, wielded the knife again.

'And not mash, for God's sake,' he begged.

Sunshine made an exasperated sound and tried again.

Leo turned his back—it was either that or wrench the knife from her—and concentrated on the salmon he'd packed as a failsafe, coating it in herbs, then laying it in a pan to fry.

Sunshine was onto the song about love biting you in the ass, throwing in the occasional excruciating lyric—and he wanted so badly to laugh it was almost painful.

Mid-song, however, *she* laughed. 'Oops—that song is just too, too, *too* much, Hideous,' she said.

Damn if he didn't want to snatch her up and kiss her.

Instead he gave her some terse instructions on trimming the crunchy green beans to go into the salad, which she did abominably.

He put water on for the pasta, then turned back to the bench.

'Next, we'll—' He stopped, hurriedly averting his eyes as Sunshine arranged the salad ingredients in a bowl. 'We'll just slide the salmon on top—' shock stop as his eyes collided with the mangled contents '—and now I'll get you to mix the dressing.'

He lined up a lemon, honey, seeded mustard, sugar, black pepper, and extra virgin olive oil.

Sunshine considered the ingredients with the utmost concentration. 'So, I need to juice the lemon, right?'

'Yes. You only need a tablespoon.'

'How much is a tablespoon?'

Repressing the telltale tic, he opened the cutlery drawer and took out a tablespoon. 'This is a tablespoon.'

'Oh. How much of everything else?'

Limit reached. 'Move out of the way. I'll do it. I put a bottle of wine in the fridge. I think—no, I *know*—I need a nice big glass of it, if you can manage to pour that. Then go around to the other side of the counter, sit on that stool and watch. You've already thrown my kitchen rhythm off so things are woefully out of order.'

'It seems very ordered to me.'

'Well, it's not.'

Sunshine shrugged, unconcerned. 'You know, I feel like one of those contestants on your show.'

A thought too ghastly to contemplate!

Sunshine slid past him on her way to the fridge, brushing against his arm. *God!* God, God, *God*! Her brand of casual friendliness, with the kisses and the random touches, was something he was not used to. At all.

He didn't like it.

Except that he kind of did.

Dinner resembled a physical battle: Sunshine leaning in; Leo leaning *way* out.

A less optimistic woman would have been daunted.

But Sunshine was almost always optimistic.

As they ate the pasta and salad they argued over assorted wedding details, from the choice of MC—*'What are you thinking to suggest anyone but yourself, Leo?'*—to the need for speeches—Sunshine: yes; Leo: no!—to whether to use social media for sharing photos and videos of the function—over Leo's dead body, apparently.

By the time the pannacotta gelato was on the table Sunshine was in 'what the hell?' mode. Seven weeks to go—they had to move things along.

'So!' she said. 'Music!'

He went deer-in-the-headlights still. 'Music.'

'Yes. Music. I hear there's no dancing, so we can scrap the DJ option.'

'Correct.'

She pursed her lips. 'So! I've located a heavy metal band. I also know a great piano accordionist—surprisingly soulful. And I've heard about an Irish trio. What about one of those options? Or maybe a big band—but did you know that a big band has fourteen instruments? And where would we put fourteen musicians? I mean, I know the restaurant is spacious, but—'

'I know what you're doing, Sunshine.'

She blinked at him, the picture of innocence—she knew because she'd practised in the mirror. 'What do you mean, Leo?'

'Suggesting horrific acts and thinking that by the time you get around to naming the option you really want I'll be so relieved I'll agree instantly.'

'But that's not true. Well…not *strictly* true. Because I *have* named what I really want. Natalie Clarke.'

'No.'

'Why not?'

'Because.'

'Because why?'

'Caleb doesn't want her there.'

'Is that the only reason? Because I can talk to Caleb.'

'It's the only reason you're going to get.'

Sunshine gave him a bemused look. 'Is this because you used to date her? You know, I'm good friends with *all* my exes.'

'I, however, am not.'

'Why not?'

Leo scooped up a spoonful of gelato. Ate it. 'I just don't do that.'

'Why not?'

'They're just not that…that kind.'

'Kind?'

'Kind of person. People. Not the kind of people I'm friends with.'

She nodded wisely. 'You're choosing wrong.'

He took another mouthful of gelato. Said nothing.

'Because you don't want someone, really,' she said. 'You're like me.' Sunshine tapped her heart. 'No room in here.'

Leo's spoon clattered into his bowl. 'I've got room. Plenty. But I want…' He stopped, looking confused.

'You want…?'

'Someone…special.'

'Special as in…?'

'As in someone to throw myself off the cliff for, leap into the abyss with,' he said, sounding goaded. 'There! Are you happy?'

'My happiness is not the issue here.'

He dragged a hand over his head. Gave a short, surprised laugh. 'I want all or nothing.'

'And Natalie didn't?'

'She wanted…the illusion. She wanted the illusion of it without the depth.'

'Oh.'

'Yes—*oh*.'

'Not that I think there's anything wrong with not wanting the depth.'

'Of *course* there's something wrong with it,' he said with asperity. 'You're wrong about the whole no-room, sex-not-love thing.'

'Each to his or her own,' Sunshine said. 'And I still don't see why Natalie can't perform at the reception. You wouldn't even have to talk to her. I could do the negotiations.'

He snorted.

'Why the snort?'

'Forget it.'

'I am *not* going to forget it.

'Look—' He stopped, shot a hand across his scalp again. 'No, I don't want to go there.'

'Well, I do!'

'Oh, for God's sake!' Leo looked at her, exasperated. 'Natalie is a bunny-boiler, okay? She would not settle for negotiating with you—she'd be aiming for me. Always, *always* me. Got it?'

Sunshine sat back in her seat. Stared. *'No!'*

'Yes!'

'But…why?'

'How the hell do I know why? I only know the what— like eating at one of my restaurants every week. Driving my staff nuts with questions about me. Sending me stuff. So just leave it, Sunshine. I know another singer. Her name's Kate. I'll give you some CDs to listen to.'

'Is she an ex?'

'No. She's just a good singer with no agenda.'

Sunshine sighed inwardly but admitted defeat. 'Fair enough.' She stretched her arms over her head and arched her back. *'Mmm.* Next time maybe you should teach me how to make paella. I love paella.'

'One problem with that plan,' Leo said. 'I am never entering a kitchen with you again.'

'Oh, that's mean.'

'Think of the poor tomatoes.'

'What was wrong with the tomatoes?'

'Other than the fact that they looked like blood-spatter from a crime scene?'

Sunshine bit her lip against a gurgle of laughter. 'What about the prosciutto? I managed to tear that the way you showed me.'

'Flayed flesh.'

'Ouch,' Sunshine said, but she was laughing. 'What about how I scooped the gelato?'

'Please! Like ooze from a wound.'

'It's a good thing I don't have any coffee, or we'd be up to poison.'

'Since I didn't see an espresso machine in that shell of a kitchen, poison sounds about right.'

Rolling her eyes, Sunshine pushed her chair back from the table. 'Well, then, I will make you some tea—something all well-bred hippies *can* do. Unless you have some words to throw at me about scalded skin. The invitation is on the coffee table, waiting for your approval, so why don't you check it out while I clear up? Something *else* I can do.'

She watched from the corner of her eye as Leo moved to the couch, sat, reached for the invitation.

He was smiling—full-on!—as he slid the pad of his thumb so gently across the card, as though it were something precious. Oh, he did look good when he smiled. It was kind of crooked, with the left side lifting up further than the right. A little rusty. And it just got her—*bang!*—right in the chest.

Fried bat, anyone?

Tearing her eyes away, Sunshine finished making the tea.

'So! Is it okay?' she asked, sliding two mugs onto the coffee table and sitting beside Leo.

He turned to her, smiled again. *Heaven!*

'It's great. The calligraphy too.'

'I guess the next step is to discuss the menu.'

Leo picked up his mug. 'I'm going with a seafood bias, given the location.'

'Uncanny! Exactly what I was thinking.'

'Canapés to start. Local oysters, freshly shucked clams

served ceviche-style, poached prawns with aioli, and hand-milked Yarra Valley caviar with *crème fraîche*.'

'*Ohhhhh...*'

'Buffalo mozzarella and semi-dried tomato on croutons, honey-roasted vegetable tartlets, and mini lamb and feta kofta'

'*Mmm...*'

'Just champagne, beer, and sparkling water—we don't need to get too fancy with the drinks to start. But any special requirements we can accommodate on request.'

'Good, because Jon's mother will insist on single malt whisky—and through *every* course. *Nothing* we say ever dissuades her.'

'Well, it's better than a line of coke with every course.'

She gaped at him. 'Line of...?'

'Natalie,' he said shortly. 'Another reason she will not be performing at the wedding. Just to be absolutely clear.'

'That's...' She waved a hand, lost.

'Anyway, moving on. The first course will be calamari, very lightly battered and deep fried, served with a trio of dipping sauces—lime and coriander, smoked jalapeno mayonnaise, and a sweet plum sauce.'

'Oh, Leo, could you teach me how to make that at least?'

'No. The main meal will be lobster, served with a lemon butter sauce and a variety of salads that I wouldn't dare describe to you.'

'Lobster! Oh.' She took a sip of tea. 'You know, Leo, I saw the most intriguing thing about lobsters on the internet.'

'Yes?' He sounded wary.

'They are actually immortal! They stay alive until they get eaten.'

'That can't be true.'

'Which means coming back as a lobster in the next life wouldn't be such a bad thing. Except...' Nose-wrinkle.

'Well, I'm not sure that when they're caught they're always killed humanely. So you might be lucky enough to live for ever—or you might get thrown into a pot of boiling water and be absolutely screaming, without even having the ability to make a sound, because some sadistic cook couldn't be bothered to kill you first.'

Leo gave a sigh brimming with long suffering. 'Okay—barramundi it is,' he said. 'Coated with lemon and caper butter and wrapped in pancetta, served with in-season asparagus.'

'That sounds divine. And so much more humane.'

'I am *not* a lobster sadist,' Leo said, sounding as if he were gritting his teeth.

'Well, of course not.'

There was the tic. 'And they are not immortal.'

'Well, they might be—who would know? And they can, a hundred per cent, live to about one hundred and forty years. Which is *almost* immortal.'

He regarded her through narrowed eyes. 'How is it you've made it to twenty-five without being murdered?'

'You're definitely watching too many crime shows.'

'Dessert,' he said firmly. 'I'm thinking about figs.'

'Figs. Oh.' Sip of tea.

'"Figs oh" *what*? Is this the fruit version of your vegetarian hang-up? Because there *will* be sugar, you know.'

'It's not th— Actually, it *is* partly that. But, more to the point, I think fig pollination is kind of disgusting.'

He had that fascinated look going on.

'Wasps,' she said.

'Wasps?'

'They burrow into the fig and lay their eggs in the fruit, then die in there. *Ergh*. And it's quite brutal, because on the way in the poor wasp can lose her wings and her antennae—it's a tight fit, I guess. Come on—you have to agree that's a bit repulsive. And sad too.'

Leo had closed his eyes. Tic, tic, tic.

A moment passed. Another. He opened his eyes and looked at her. 'So, we'll serve a variation on the glacé I made for you at Q Brasserie—perhaps with a rose syrup base. And, because it's a wedding, some Persian confetti.'

Sunshine beamed at him. 'That's just perfect.'

'And remember I know your modus operandi, Sunshine Smart-Ass.'

'But I don't have one of those!'

Leo simply put up the 'stop' hand. 'For the non-seafood-lovers there will be ricotta tortellini with burnt-sage butter sauce as an alternative first course, and either chargrilled lime and mint chicken or a Moroccan-style chickpea tagine for your fellow commune dwellers for the main course.'

'Oh, even the chickpea thing sounds good. Because chickpeas are sort of like the meat of vegetables, don't you think?'

'No, I don't.'

'What about the cake?'

'Four options: traditional fruit cake, salted caramel—which we can do with either a chocolate or butterscotch base—or coconut.'

'Oh! *Oh!* Could we do one of those cake-tasting things? You know, where you sit around and try before you buy? I would *so* love to do a cake-tasting.'

'For the love of God, can't we just ask the guys what they want?'

'What would be the fun in that?' Sunshine asked, mystified.

Leo ran that hand over his head. 'I'll talk to Anton—he's my *pâtissier.*'

'And I have the most amazing idea for the decoration. Kind of Art Deco—my current favourite thing. Square tiers, decorated with hand-cut architectural detailing, in white and shades of grey, with painted silver accents. Wait a moment—I've got a photo.'

Sunshine leapt off the couch and raced into her office, grabbed the photo and raced back out. 'What do you think?' she asked, thrusting it at him.

But Leo was looking past her into the office.

She'd forgotten to close the door.

'Oh,' she said, seeing through his eyes the green-striped wallpaper, the reproduction antique furniture painted in vivid blues, reds, and yellows, the framed prints of lusciously coloured shoes through the ages hung on the walls.

The urn with Moonbeam's ashes. In his direct line of sight.

Oh, no! Sunshine raced back to close the door.

'So!' she said, her heart beating hard as she came back to sit beside him. 'So! The cake.'

'I'll talk to Anton,' Leo said absently, still looking at the closed door.

Sunshine decided drastic action was needed—just to make sure he didn't ask to actually go in there.

Going with gut feeling—and, all right, secret desire—she hugged him.

He seemed to freeze for a moment, and then his arms came around her. He gathered her in for one moment. She heard, felt him inhale slowly.

Wow! He was actually touching her! Voluntarily! Except that this wasn't exactly touching—it was more. Better! Absorbing! He was absorbing her! Talk about exclamation mark overload!

His arms were so hard. So was his chest. It should have felt like being pulled against a brick wall…and yet there was something yielding about him. His hand came up, touched the back of her head, fingers sliding into her hair.

Good. But Sunshine wanted more. Much more.

She pulled out of his arms, sat back, looked at him. 'I don't know how you're going to take this, Leo,' she said, 'but I want to have sex with you.'

CHAPTER FIVE

LEO STARED. COULDN'T so much as blink.

A minute ticked by.

She was waiting for him to speak, her head tilted—the curious bird look.

Had he heard correctly?

Had Sunshine Smart just told him, taking matter-of-factness to the level of an art form, that she wanted to have *sex* with him? And that she didn't know how he'd *take* that confession?

'What did you just say?' he asked at last, and his voice sounded as though he hadn't used it for a month.

'Just that I want to have sex with you.' Sunshine pursed her lips, considering him. 'Are you shocked? Horrified? Appalled? Because you don't look interested.'

'Gary. Ben. Marco.' He listed them without elaborating.

'Gary, Ben and Marco?' she said, as though she had no idea what he was getting at.

'How many lovers do you need?'

She gave him an *Aha!* kind of look, then said simply, 'Okay, I'll tell you. I'm not sleeping with any of them. I'm not sleeping with anyone. I *hoped* there would be a spark with Gary, but it never developed. Ben? Twice. But that's ancient history, and we won't talk about his addiction to cheesy love songs in the bedroom.'

Momentary distraction. '*Ben* and cheesy love songs? What *is* it with people and cheesy love songs?'

'I know—it's crazy! So, of course, it was never going to go anywhere. Marco—well, that would be a cold day in hell.' She looked at him. 'But there's no need to talk it to death. If you're not interested let's just move on. We have a tough seven weeks ahead, and there's just not enough time for us to go through an awkward phase.'

'How the hell am I supposed to *move on*?' Leo asked, incredulous.

'I said I wanted to have sex with you—not that I wanted to marry you. And only up to four times, which is my limit.' She looked at him thoughtfully. 'You don't suffer from priapism by any chance, do you?'

'From *what*?'

'Guess not. Well, then—are you, perhaps, a virgin who's signed some sort of pledge?'

'No, of course I'm not a *virgin*.'

'Well, I don't know why you say *"of course"* like that. There are more virgins out there than you realise. In fact I read on the internet that—'

'And what do you mean, only up to four times?' he asked, jumping in before she could give him virgin facts. Because he did *not* want virgin facts.

'Any more than four times and things get messy. You know—emotional. If you don't want to develop a relationship it's best to set a limit. And I don't. Want to develop a relationship. I mean; I *do* want to set a limit. Hmm, you're giving me that look.'

'What look?'

'That *she's insane* look.'

'That's because you are. Insane.'

'I'm just sensible, Leo. Men do this stuff all the time. Pick up a girl in a seedy bar—not that we're in a seedy bar, of course, but you get the picture—then race her off to the bedroom, then do the I'll-call-you routine when they have no *intention* of calling. So why can't I? Well, not the I'll-call-you thing—I would never say I'd call someone and then not do it. And there really is no *reason* not to call. Regardless of whether you want to have sex with them again. Because you had to like them in *some* way to get into bed with them in the first place, so you should want to see where the friendship goes, shouldn't you? The sex part is kind of incidental—because sex is just…well, *sex*.'

Pause.

Thank God. Because his head was spinning.

'I guess what I'm saying,' she continued, unabashed, 'is that it's better to be up-front about what you want— just sex, just friendship, sex and then friendship. Whatever! But no tragic *I love you* just to wring an orgasm out of someone.'

'What if you *do* fall in love?'

'I won't. I never have. And I never will. I told you before: I won't let myself care that much.'

'So you're saying Jonathan and Caleb should give up the idea of marriage and just have sex?'

Her face softened. 'No, I'm happy for them. And I know the love thing works for lots of people—my parents are a prime example. It just doesn't work for me.'

'How do you know if you've never been there?'

'Haven't we already had this discussion?'

'Not thoroughly enough, Sunshine.'

Another pause. 'All right, then. The fact is I'm too… intense. I feel things too intensely.'

'Not thoroughly *enough*,' he repeated.

She bit her lower lip, worried it between her teeth. And then, haltingly, she said, 'I didn't recover—not properly— from my sister's death.' The tears were there, being blinked furiously away. 'I can't describe it. The agony. The… *agony*.'

'That's a different kind of love,' he said, but gently.

'A different *kind*, yes. But the *depth*… I just think it's safe, for me, to splash in the shallows—not to swim out of my depth.' She laughed, but there was no humour in it. 'Huh. A line of coke and I'd be Natalie.'

'You're nothing like Natalie. And you already have strong, deep ties—to Jon, to your parents…'

'Yes. I love Jon, and I love my parents. But it was too late to do anything about them; they were already here.' Small tap over the heart. 'I'm just limiting further damage.' She tried to smile. 'And, anyway, the in-love kind of love would be the *most* damaging. Because I know how I'd be in love. Kill for him, die for him…'

'The kind I want.'

'The kind you *say* you want, anyway. Into the abyss, off the cliff. But you'll see, when you've fallen into the abyss, that there's anguish there—in the fear of losing the one you love, or even just losing the love. And I can't—won't—go through that. Because next time I just don't know how I—' She stopped. Blew out a breath. 'Let's not go there. Let's just keep the focus on sex.'

Leo could hear muted noises from outside floating up from the street. Traffic. A laugh. A shout. But inside it was quiet. 'So you've restricted your lovers to a four-night term ever since Moonbeam died? And none of them ever wanted to take things further?'

'They knew it was never going to happen. And I've managed to stay good friends with all of them despite that—which is more than you can say. Well, all of them bar one.'

'And what went wrong with him?'

'He just doesn't like women dictating the terms, so we didn't even make it to the first…what would you call it?… assignation? Yes, assignation.' She did the curious bird thing. 'I'm guessing you're in his camp.'

Leo had no idea, at that point, *what* he thought. But he didn't like Sunshine telling him which camp he was in, thank you very much! 'No, I'm not in that camp.'

Sunshine smiled. 'So! Are you saying you *would* consider it, Leo? Sex, I mean?'

'No, I'm not saying that either.'

Another smile. 'Shall we try a little experiment, then?'

Long silence. And then, 'What kind of experiment?'

'I'll kiss you and you can see how that makes you feel.'

He opened his mouth to say no.

But Sunshine didn't let him get that far.

She simply moved so she was straddling him. She undulated, once, against him, and he thought he would explode on the spot. *Holy hell.* Then she settled, cocooning him between her forearms as she gripped the back of the sofa, one hand on each side of his head. Jonquils. Red silk. Heat and buzz and glow. She dipped her head, nipped his lower lip.

'No, that wasn't the kiss—that was me signalling my intention, as I promised to do.' She smiled. 'So! Ready?'

Any thought of denying her went straight out of his head like a shot of suddenly liberated steam. Leo gripped her hips, ground her against him, wanting her to feel his raging erection—although he didn't know why, unless her form of insanity was contagious—and took over, devouring her mouth with a hard, savaging kiss.

Her mouth was amazing. Open, luscious, drawing him in. His tongue, hot and agile, swept the roof of her mouth, the insides of her cheeks, under her super-sexy top lip. The tart sweetness of the lemony tea was delicious when it was licked from inside her. He could feel that slight gap between her front teeth. He moved his hands, cupped her face to keep her there, just *there*, so he could taste more deeply.

He could feel his heart thundering. Became aware that her hands were now fisted in his shirt as she rocked against him, forced her mouth and his wider still. She was whimpering, alternately jamming her tongue into his mouth and then licking his lips. And rocking, rocking, *rocking* against him until he thought he'd go mad with wanting.

Then her hands were moving between them, fingers plucking at the button of his jeans, which opened in a 'thank God' moment, then sliding his zipper down, freeing him.

'Ah…' he gasped, pulling his mouth away so he could breathe, try to think. But it was no use. He had to kiss her again.

She reeled him back in, pulled him closer, angled him so that when she lay back, flattened on the couch, he was on top of her.

Then his hands were there, pulling up the red silk. Up, up, up. So he could touch her skin, which was like satin. No, not satin—warmer than satin. Velvet…like velvet. His fingers slid higher, closer. He didn't want to wait—couldn't wait—*had* to feel her, to be in her the fastest way he could get there.

Without disengaging his mouth from hers, he plunged his fingers into her. Again. She arched into the touch.

She didn't speak, but breathed out words. His name. *'Leo. Yes, yes. Leo…'*

And then it wasn't his fingers but him needing to be there, buried in her as deep as he could go, panting, straining, wanting this, wanting *her*, silently demanding that she come for him. For *him*.

He felt her body tightening, straining, heard his name explode from her lips as the orgasm gripped her. He pushed hard into her, and kissed her drugging mouth again as he followed her into a life-draining release.

They lay there, connected, in a tangle of clothes, spent.

After a long moment Sunshine gave a shaky laugh. 'That was some kiss,' she said.

But Leo didn't feel like laughing. He felt like diving into her again...and also, contrarily, like getting the hell away from her. From her rules. Her determination to fix him in the place where she wanted him. Just where she wanted him. No further.

Awkwardly, he disengaged himself from her body.

Sunshine sat up, pushing at her hair with one unsteady hand and at her dress with the other. She looked like the cat that had got the cream.

Infuriating.

Mechanically, Leo adjusted his clothing. He was appalled to realise he hadn't even *seen* her during that mad sexual scramble. Did that make him some kind of depraved, desperate sex fiend, that he'd treated her body like a receptacle? But then, he hadn't really *needed* to see her to know very well that it was her driving him wild—so wild he hadn't been able to think past the need to be inside her.

'Are you sorry?' Sunshine asked softly.

She was watching him with wary concern.

'No. Yes. I don't know.'

Tiny laugh. 'Multiple *choice*? How...comprehensive.'

He stood abruptly, shoved his hands in his pockets, not trusting where he'd put them otherwise.

'Leo, don't go. We have to talk about this.'

He shook his head.

She got to her feet, took his hand. 'You will get all angsty if you leave now, because it happened so fast and we weren't expecting it to go like that. We can't have angst; we have too much to do. Come on, sit with me—let's make sure we can get back to normal before you go.'

How did you talk yourself back to *normal* after that?

How did a kiss turn into rip-your-heart-out sex in one blinding flash of a moment? And that complete loss of control... It had never happened to him before. No condom. Not even a *thought* of one! He was shaken. Badly.

And—God!—she was still holding his hand, and he was rubbing his thumb over her knuckles, and he hadn't even noticed he was doing it. He didn't *do* that touchy-feely stuff.

He dropped her hand and stepped back. 'You're dangerous, Sunshine,' he said.

She looked startled. 'It's not like I'm a black widow spider or a praying mantis.'

'What the—? All right, I think I get the black widow spider. But what's so dangerous about a praying mantis?'

Her eyes lit. 'Oh, it's really interesting! Praying mantises can only have sex once the female rips off the male's head. Imagine! At least you still have your head.'

Leo felt his lips twitch. But he was *not* going to laugh. It was not a funny situation. It was an *angsty* one. Angsty? God.

'On that note, I'm going,' he said.

'But we have to talk.'

'Not now. Meet me… I don't know… Tomorrow. At the Rump & Chop Grill. Five o'clock. It's only a few blocks from here. I'll send someone for my kitchen gear in the morning.'

'All right, tomorrow,' she agreed, and walked with him to the door, where she stopped him. 'Leo, just so you can think about it before then…I want to have sex with you again. We have up to three more opportunities, and there doesn't seem to be a reason not to use them. We just need to schedule them so we don't get distracted from the wedding preparations.'

He was staring again. Couldn't help it.

'Far be it from me to distract you, Sunshine,' he said.

So!

Yowzer!

As Sunshine wallowed in her bubble bath, lathering

herself with her favourite jonquil-scented soap, she pondered what had happened.

It sure hadn't been a cheesy-love-song experience. More like heavy metal—hard and loud and banging. But maybe with a clash of cymbal thrown in. She smiled, stretched, almost purred.

She knew she would be reliving the sex for an hour or so—that was par for the course. The sexual post-mortem…a normal female ritual. Remembering exactly what had happened, what had been murmured, who'd put what where.

But at four o'clock in the morning she was still trying to piece it together and parcel it off. She wondered if the difficulty was that she didn't have a precise anatomical memory of the experience. She couldn't recall everything that had been said, every touch, every kiss. She just had an… *awareness*. That it had been so gloriously *right*, somehow.

Which was strange. Because technically it shouldn't have been that memorable. They hadn't taken off their clothes; Leo hadn't touched her breasts—which she'd always counted as her best assets—and he hadn't even bothered to look at the goods before plunging in—which was a waste of her painfully acquired Brazilian!

But none of that seemed to matter because the *can't wait* roughness of it had been more seductive than an hour of foreplay. She hadn't needed foreplay. Hadn't wanted finesse. Hadn't thought about condoms. Hadn't thought about anything. She'd been so hot, so ready for him.

She wondered—if that rough-and-ready first time was any indication—just how magnificent the next time would be.

Because there *would* be a next time. She was going to make sure of it.

TO: Jonathan Jones
FROM: Sunshine Smart
SUBJECT: Party news

Isn't the menu great? Leo=food genius.

Just the wedding cake to go. I'd tell you the options, but if you chose one I wouldn't get my cake-tasting, which you know I've always wanted to do.

Leo cooked the most amazing meal last night. He is so different from the men I usually meet. More mature, steadier. Kind of conservative—I like that.

His hair is coming along too.
Sunny xxx

TO: Sunshine Smart
FROM: Jonathan Jones
SUBJECT: Do not sleep with Leo Quartermaine
DO NOT!!!!! That would be all kinds of hideous.
Jon

TO: Jonathan Jones
FROM: Sunshine Smart
SUBJECT: Re: Do not sleep with Leo Quartermaine
Oops! Too late!

But how did you know? And why hideous?
Sunny

TO: Sunshine Smart
FROM: Jonathan Jones
SUBJECT: Re:Re: Do not sleep with Leo Quartermaine
OH, MY FREAKING GOD, SUNNY!!!!!!!!

How do I know? For starters because every second word you're writing is 'Leo'!

He's not the type to enjoy the ride then buddy up at the end. You know his parents were drug addicts, right? You know he basically dragged Caleb through that hell and into a proper life?

He's a tough hombre, not a poncy investment banker,

soulful embalmer or saucy hairdresser. This is not a man for you to play with.

Let's talk tonight—10 p.m. your time. With video. No arguments.

Jon

Sunshine got to the Rump & Chop Grill fifteen minutes early. Although it was part of a pub, it had a separate entrance on a side road—which was locked.

She decided against knocking and inveigling her way inside to wait. That would have been her usual approach. But Leo already had one bunny-boiler on his tail, as well as being in a state about last night, so it was probably best not to look *too* enthusiastic.

Fortunately there was a café across the road, where she could wait and watch for him. Which would give her time to think.

Because Jon's email had thrown her.

The thing with Leo was a simple sexual arrangement. No need for concern on *anyone's* part.

So he'd had drug addict parents? And, no, of course she hadn't known that! How could she have, unless someone had told her? And why did it make a difference anyway? Unless Leo was a drug addict himself—and given his obvious disgust over his ex-girlfriend's coke habit that seemed unlikely.

Did Jon think the fact that Leo and Caleb had navigated a hellish childhood would put her off him? It clearly hadn't put Jon off Caleb, so why the double standard? And Caleb had come through unscathed. He was a terrific guy—very different from his brother, of course—at least from what she'd seen during their internet chats. Funny and charming and *out there*. Not that Leo wasn't also terrific, but he certainly didn't have Caleb's lightness of spirit.

But it was to Leo's credit, wasn't it, if he was the one

who'd dragged them both out of the gutter? She admired him *more*, not less, because of it. Liked him more.

Okay—*that* could be a problem. She didn't actually *want* to admire or like him more, because admiration and liking could lead to other things. And what she wanted was to keep things just as they were.

Hot man, in her bed, up to three more times. Finish.

As she would tell Jon, very firmly, tonight.

So! For now she would stop thinking about Leo's horrible childhood and concentrate on the wedding reception. *Not* that Jon deserved to have her fussing over it after that email, but...well, she loved Jon. And she was going to make the bastard's wedding reception perfect if it killed her.

While she sat in the café, disgruntled, sipping a coffee she didn't even want, she scanned the checklist. Having the function at South was brilliant, but it did add an extra task: finding accommodation for people who wouldn't want to drive back to Sydney. She figured they would need two options—cheap and cheerful, and sumptuous luxury. If she could get it sorted quickly, hotel booking details could be sent out with the invitations. She was sure Leo wouldn't want to traipse through hotels with her, so she would shoot down the coast herself and just keep him in the loop via email.

Right. The next urgent thing on the list was what Leo was wearing.

At least it was urgent from *her* perspective, because his shoe design hinged on it. And so did her outfit.

She was dying to wear her new 1930s-style dress in platinum charmeuse. It looked almost molten. Hugging her curves—all right, a little dieting might be required—in an elegantly simple torso wrap before tumbling in an understated swirl to the ground. It even had a divine little train. And she could wear her adorable gunmetal satin peep-toes with the retro crystal buckles.

But there was no good glamming to the hilt if Leo was going to play it down. And so far, aside from his pristine chef's whites, she hadn't seen an inclination for dressing up. Just jeans, T-shirts, sweaters. Good shoes, but well-worn and casual.

She heard a roar, and a second later a motorbike—it had to be his—pulled up outside the restaurant. One economical swing of his leg and he was off, reefing his helmet from his head.

Her heart jumped into her throat and her stomach whooshed.

Nope.

This was not going to work.

She couldn't think about clothes or shoes or hotels when he was still riding that damned bike. She was going to have talk to him about it. *Again.* And again and again. Until he got rid of it.

She straightened her spine and set her jaw. She was *not* to going to spend the next seven weeks dreading his death on the road! She stashed the wedding folder into her brief-case, threw some money on the table and exited the café.

Leo saw Sunshine the moment she stepped onto the foot-path, his eyes snap-locking on to her from across the road. She looked good, as usual, wearing a winter green skirt suit that fitted her as snugly as the skin on a peach, and high-heeled chocolate-brown pumps.

'Leo, I have to talk to you,' she said.

He waited for that smacking kiss to land on his cheek.

But his cheek remained unsullied. She was clearly agitated—too agitated to bother with the kiss.

Well, good, he thought savagely. She *should* be agitated after last night. *He* certainly was.

'Yep, that was the plan,' Leo said, and unlocked the door.

Sunshine was practically humming with impatience as he relocked the door and escorted her to a table in the middle of the restaurant.

'I'll just check the kitchen and I'll be back,' he said, and almost smiled at the way her face pinched. *Yeah, cool your jets, Sunshine Smart-Ass, because you are not in control here.*

Not that that he was necessarily in control himself, but she didn't have to know that he hadn't been able to think straight since last night—let alone make a decision on her offer of three more pulse-ricocheting bouts of sex.

He was a man—ergo, it was an attractive proposition. But sex just for the sake of sex? Well, not to be arrogant, but he had his pick of scores of women if that was all he wanted. All right, the sex last night had been fairly spectacular, although hardly his most selfless performance, but it was still a commodity in abundant supply.

So, did he want more than sex from Sunshine?

Even as the question darted into his head he rejected it with a big *hell no.*

He didn't like perky and he didn't like breezy. Perky and breezy—AKA Sunshine Smart—were synonyms for negligent in his book. Choosing the shallows over the depths, wallowing in the past instead of confronting life head-on, the whole sex-only mantra. That kind of devil-may-care irresponsibility described his deadbeat parents, who'd not only offered up their bodies and any scrap of dignity for a quick score, but had been so hopeless they'd dropped dead of overdoses within days of each other, orphaning two sons.

Okay, the 'poor little orphans' bit was overcooked, because he and Caleb had stopped relying on them years before their deaths—but the principle remained.

So, no—he did *not* want more than sex from Sunshine.

And he didn't need *just* sex from her either.

All he needed from cheery, perky, breezy, ditzy Sunshine Smart was a hassle-free seven weeks of wedding preparations, after which he would set his compass and sail on.

Pretty clear, then.

Decision made.

Sex was off the table.

And the couch. And the bed. And wherever else she'd been planning on frying his gonads.

And he would enjoy telling her. Quickly—because he'd made this decision several times throughout the day, then gone back to re-mulling the options, and enough was enough.

But when he sat down across from Sunshine, all primed to give her the news, she forestalled him by saying urgently, 'Leo, you need to get rid of that motorbike. It's too dangerous.'

He took a moment to switch gears because he hadn't been expecting that. Sex, yes. Clothes, yes. Shoes, fine. But not the motorbike again.

'Yes, well, as it's my body on it, you can safely leave the decision about my transportation to me.'

'There's no "safely" about it.'

He looked at her closely, saw that there was nothing cheery-perky-breezy-ditzy in her face.

'Whoa,' he said. 'Let's take a step back. What's really behind this?'

'I want you to be alive for the wedding—that's all.'

'That's not all, Sunshine. Tell me, or this discussion is over.'

She dashed a hand across her fringe, pushing it aside impatiently. Looked at him, hard and bright and on edge, and then, 'My sister,' exploded from her mouth.

Leo waited. His hands had clenched into fists. Because

he wanted to touch her again. He felt a little trickle of something suspiciously like fear shiver down his spine.

'You may think it's none of my business—and it's not, strictly speaking,' she said. 'But it's not my way to stand aside and *not* say or do something when death is staring someone in the face. How could I live with myself if I didn't interfere and then something happened to you?'

'And you go around giving this lecture to everyone on a motorbike?'

'No, of course not—only to people I...' She faltered there. 'People I...know,' she finished lamely, putting up her chin.

Leo considered her for a long moment. *Not buying it.* 'Your sister. I want the whole story. I assumed...an illness. Wrong, obviously. I should have asked.'

'I didn't want you to ask. I didn't *let* you ask. Because to talk about that...to you, with your bike...it would have been a link. And I couldn't... But now...' Pause...deep breath while she gathered herself together. 'Sorry. I'm not making sense. I'll be clearer. Moonbeam had a motorbike. She crashed and she died. I was on the back and I survived. We were the cliché identical twins—inseparable. And then suddenly, just like...like...' She clicked her fingers. 'I was...'

The words just petered out. He saw her swallow, as if she had a sharp rock in her throat.

'Alone?' he finished for her.

'Yes. Alone.'

He waited a heartbeat. Two. Three.

She kept her eyes on his face, but apparently she wasn't intending to add anything.

'Sunshine,' he said softly, 'death is *not* staring me in the face. I'm not a teenage hothead burning up the road. I'm thirty. And I'm careful.'

'What if someone not so careful knocks you off?'

'Is that what happened? Did someone run your sister down?'

She shook her head, looking as if she would burst from frustration. 'No. She was going too fast. Missed the corner.'

Leo ran a hand over his head. Tried to find something to say. He was scared to open his mouth in case he promised her that, yes, he would give up the one carefree thing he allowed himself. They'd known each other for one week: she couldn't really care—had said she *wouldn't* care. And he would *not* be seduced into sacrificing his bike by the thought that she did.

'Look,' he started, and then stopped, ran a hand over his head again. 'It's not your job, Sunshine, to worry about me.'

'But I *do* worry about you. *Please*, Leo.'

There was a loud crashing sound from the kitchen. 'I have to check that.' Leo got to his feet, but then he paused, looking down at her. 'I shouldn't have started this. Not here, where there are too many distractions. Go home, and we'll pick it up another time.'

'I'm eating here tonight,' Sunshine said. 'And, no, I am *not* turning into a stalker. I have a date. Iain.'

His eyes narrowed. 'The hairdresser? The ex, who's now just a friend?'

'That's right.'

'As long as it *is* ex. Because while you and I are sleeping together—even if it is only four times—there isn't going to be anyone else in the picture. Got it? I'm not into sharing.' He heard the words come out of his mouth but couldn't quite believe they had. *Okay*, so he'd changed his mind and sex was back on, apparently.

'Well, of course!' Sunshine said. 'Actually, the main reason I asked him to come tonight was to check your head.'

'Check my head?' Leo repeated, not getting it.

'To make sure it's going to be long enough—not your head, because obviously that's not growing any more, but your hair.'

'He is *not* checking my head, Sunshine.'

That damned nose-wrinkle. 'But I think—'

'No,' Leo said, and strode into the kitchen.

Where he burst out laughing and stopped half the staff in their tracks.

'What?' he asked.

But nobody was brave enough to answer.

Sunshine did not enjoy dinner.

Not that the food wasn't great—because who couldn't love a Wagyu beef burger with Stilton, and chilli salt fries on the side?

And Iain had brought sketches of the most fabulous hairstyle for the wedding. Finger waves pinned at the base of the neck and secured with a gorgeous hairclip. Her fringe would be swept aside—*please* let it be long enough—and similarly clipped above her ear.

But neither the food nor the sketches was enough to take her mind off that damned motorbike, and the fact that Leo, who was so sensible, didn't seem to understand that it had to go.

So she fumed. And, because she'd always supposed she didn't carry the fuming gene, the unwelcome evidence that she could get as wound up as a garden variety maniac bothered her.

They'd had sex. That didn't mean she had a hold over him, of course, but it made him...well...someone more important than a casual acquaintance.

She became aware that Iain was sing-songing her name softly from across the table and snapped her attention back to where it should have been all night.

'That's better,' he said.

'Sorry, Iain. I haven't been good company tonight.'

'You're always good company, Sunny.'

She smiled at him. 'You're too nice.'

'Nice?' He gave a short, almost bitter laugh. 'Was that the limiter?'

'What? No!' She looked at him, dismayed. 'The problem was—is always—that I just don't want…that.'

'Someone's going to change your mind, Sunny—and all of us who have been forced to accept the limit are going to be mighty annoyed.'

All of us? Good Lord! 'You make it sound like there's a zombie camp of men out there, slavishly doing my bidding! And nobody is going to get annoyed—because I'm *not* changing my mind, ever. *And* I also happen to know you're dating Louise, so— Oh!'

She stopped abruptly. Stared past Iain.

Because Natalie Clarke, accompanied by a pretty guy vaguely familiar as a model—Rob-something—was being seated at the next table.

Natalie was stunning. Gold skin, glorious copper hair, perfect rosebud mouth, pale grey eyes. She was superslender, wearing a tight black leather skirt and a cropped black jacket. Black suede boots that made Sunshine green with envy.

Natalie shrugged out of her jacket to reveal a teensy white top; a black demi-bra was clearly visible underneath.

Iain's eyes went straight to the mother lode!

Sunshine, swallowing a laugh, kicked Iain under the table. *Bolt-ons*, she mouthed at him.

So? He mouthed back, and the laugh erupted after all.

Natalie, venom in her grey eyes, looked sharply, suspiciously, over at Sunshine and Iain.

Oh. That was just *nasty.* Imagine if Natalie ever got wind of what she'd done with Leo last night! Crime scene for sure—blood spatter, flayed flesh, ooze, *and* poison, and possibly a meat cleaver in there as well!

Then Sunshine noticed the tattooed butterflies flitting down Natalie's arms, and laughed again before she could stop herself.

Oops. *Extra* venom. And not much of a sense of humour, obviously.

Sunshine shifted her attention back to Iain and made a valiant effort to ignore Natalie—but it was impossible not to hear the overly loud one-way conversation from Natalie to Rob-the-model. All about Leo!

Blah-blah…so boring that Leo never, ever cooked for people outside his restaurants. *Ha! Prosciutto fettuccine, anyone?* Blah-blah…swank parties with Leo. Blah-blah… celebrities she and Leo had met. Blah-blah…she and Leo, part of the scene. *And who said 'the scene' with a straight face?* Blah-blah, blah-*blah*!

Natalie was pushing food around her plate as she talked; Rob was at least eating, but he was also smirking. *Smirking*—was that the most infuriating facial expression in the world?

The two of them would intermittently disappear to the bathroom, then come back talking too fast and too loud. When they disappeared for the fourth time Iain mimed coke-sniffing and Sunshine grimaced.

Natalie and Rob returned to the table and within moments were back on topic: Leo. And then, clear as a bell, 'I'll take Leo back when I'm ready—because, no matter what, he's good in bed.'

Tittering laugh from Rob.

People at about six different tables were staring at Natalie, entranced.

Sunshine felt her blood pressure shoot up. If she wasn't a pacifist she would want to slap Natalie for doing this to Leo—and in his own restaurant, dammit! Sunshine's heart was racing, her brain fizzing. She felt light-headed. She was going to have to do something to stop this.

'Really, *really* good,' Natalie continued, taking in her audience, 'which is kind of psycho, because he can't even touch you unless he's fu—'

Sunshine let out a loud, long peal of exaggerated laughter, drawing all eyes. She felt like a prize idiot, and Iain was obviously uncomfortable, but it was the only option she could immediately think of to shut Natalie up.

Sunshine was racking her brain for a way to proceed when Rob solved the dilemma by jumping to his feet and clutching at his neck.

Natalie stared ineffectually at her choking date.

Someone called out for a doctor.

The manager was racing to the kitchen.

Two diffident waiters approached the table, probably hoping someone would get there before them.

The diners—apparently not a doctor amongst them—seemed frozen. No movement. Just watching.

Sunshine got to her feet with a sinking heart. On the bright side, this dramatic development had shut Natalie up. On the not so bright side, Sunshine suspected she was about to star in the next scene. She hovered for a few seconds. *Please someone else help...please.* But—nope! Sunshine sighed. So be it.

Focusing her mind, Sunshine strode to the table. 'Out of the way,' she said, pushing past a still gaping Natalie.

Sunshine thumped Rob on the back. *Nothing.* Again. Once more.

Nope. Whatever was lodged in his throat wasn't going to be beaten out of him. Rob wasn't coughing, wasn't making a sound; he was just turning blue. His eyes stared, entreating. His hands tugged at his shirt collar.

Okay, here goes. Quickly, calmly, Sunshine moved behind him, wrapped her arms around him and placed a fist between his ribcage and where she guessed his navel was. Then she covered the fist with her other hand and gave one sharp tug upwards and inwards.

A piece of meat came flying out of Rob's mouth and he staggered, grabbing at his chair, dragging in breaths.

The restaurant broke into spontaneous applause and Sunshine felt her face heat.

Thank God the waiters were now taking control.

She started to return to her table and saw Leo standing just outside the kitchen. He was staring at her as though he'd just witnessed the Second Coming.

Sunshine couldn't remember ever being so embarrassed.

She was almost relieved when Natalie's squeal snagged his attention.

His eyes widened, then narrowed as they returned to Sunshine. Not happy!

Sunshine would have laughed if she hadn't felt so shaken. What on earth did he believe had just happened? That she and Natalie had been having a friendly chat while Rob stood there choking? Maybe that Sunshine was persuading Natalie, mid-Heimlich manoeuvre, to sing at the wedding reception against Leo's express wishes?

At this point Sunshine would prefer to hire *herself* to warble a few off-key songs!

She was almost glad when Natalie, squealing again, rushed towards Leo and threw herself into his arms. Leo, looking frazzled, backed into the kitchen, pulling Natalie with him.

Frazzle away, you idiot, Sunshine said in her head, and quickly returned to Iain.

'You're amazing,' he said, standing to pull out her chair.

'Anyone could have done it,' she said dismissively. 'I'm just glad I didn't break any of his ribs—that's the main danger. And I don't want to sit, Iain. I want to go home. I have another high drama to get through tonight: a video call with Jon.'

'Why high drama?'

Sunshine sighed. 'You're not the only one worried about the zombies.'

'Jon, you're wrong.'

Those were the first words Sunshine had managed to edge into the conversation since her initial 'Hello' three minutes earlier.

Not that 'conversation' described the incendiary soliloquy Jon had been delivering, which covered her unsatisfactory outlook on life, her ill-preparedness to deal with a man of Leo's darkness, a disjointed reminder to ensure she was taking precautions—which caused her a momentary pang of guilt about the unprecedented lack of a condom last night, although she *was* on the pill and that had to count for something—and the general benefits of not actively courting disaster.

'No, Sunshine, I'm not wrong,' Jon said, and seemed ready to relaunch.

Sunshine headed him off by jamming her fingers in her ears. She raised her eyebrows, waiting. And at last he smiled.

She removed her fingers from her ears. 'This is not worth so much anxiety, Jonathan.'

'I'm worried about you, Sunny. About the way you've been living—no, only half living—since...'

She held her breath. Watched as Jonathan hesitated...

'Ever since Moon, Sunny,' he continued, but more gently. 'This four-times-only thing. The blocking yourself off from anything more. It's not *you*!'

'Yes, it is.'

'It's not.' Sigh. 'I know I'm wasting my breath.' Another sigh. 'Well, you will not be able to dictate terms to Leo

Quartermaine. Look, Leo is going to be my brother-in-law, and you're like a sister to me. I need you two to like each other. Calmly, rationally, *like* each other.'

'I'm always friends with the men I've slept with.'

'He is not like the others.'

She rolled her eyes. The zombie camp! 'There aren't that many of them, you know!'

'I know Sunshine—you talk a good game, but you don't fool me. You never have. Sleeping with a guy is the exception, not the rule. But, whether it's two or ten or a hundred guys, Leo is not like them and he will not be your friend at the end. There are other men in Sydney, and a ridiculous number of them seem happy to have you lead them around by their sex organs. Why did you have to pick Leo?'

'It kind of— He kind of— Look, the situation picked itself. That's all.'

'You mean you had no control over it? Neither of you?'

Sunshine thought back to last night. The way 'no-touch' Leo had gathered her in when she'd given him that one hug. How she'd melted just from the feel of his fingers in her hair. The way the kiss had spiralled…

'Apparently not, Jonathan.'

'This is bad, Sunny.'

'I promise not to let it interfere with the wedding.'

'You can't promise that. There are two of you.'

'I'm not going to start asking your permission before sleeping with someone,' she said, exasperated.

Pause. Silence. Jon looked morose.

'Jon?'

More silence.

'Jon—where does that leave us?'

'It leaves us, very unsatisfactorily, at loggerheads,' he said. 'And while we're there I'm going to raise the other subject you hate. Where are Moonbeam's ashes, Sunshine?'

Sunshine stiffened. 'They are in the urn, here in my office, where they've always been. Want to see them?'

'Don't be flippant. Not about this. She'd hate it, Sunny. You know she would. When are you going to do it?'

Sunshine managed a, 'Soon.' But it wasn't easy getting the word out of a suddenly clogged throat.

'You've been saying that for two years.'

'Soon,' she repeated. 'But now I have to go. I have to finish the new handbag designs.'

'I'll keep asking.'

'I will do it. Just…not yet.'

'I love you, Sunny,' Jon said, looking so sad it tore at Sunshine's heart. 'But this isn't fair. Not on Moon. Not on your parents. Not on you. You've got to let yourself get over her death.'

'I…can't. I can't, Jon.'

'You have to.' Another sigh. 'We'll speak soon.'

Sunshine signed off.

Work. She would work for a while.

But half an hour later she was still sitting there, staring at the urn that held Moonbeam's ashes. The urn was centred very precisely on top of the bureau Sunshine had painted in her sister's favourite colour—'cobalt dazzle', Moon had called it.

Sunny tapped at the computer, found her list of Moonbeam's favourite beaches. The options she'd chosen for scattering the ashes.

But not one of the options felt right. Not one!

She put her head on the desk and cried.

When Leo left the restaurant, a little after midnight, he intended to ride home, throw down a large brandy, think about life, and go to sleep.

What a night. Sunshine. Natalie. And the Heimlich manoeuvre.

The bloody Heimlich manoeuvre.

Just when he needed so badly to think of Sunshine as frippery and irresponsible she had to go and save someone's life—and then look surprised when people applauded her for it. The difference between Sunshine's calm, embarrassed heroism and Natalie's ineffectual hysterics had been an eye-opener of epic proportions.

And it had come after the Moonbeam story, which had already had his heart lurching around in his chest like a drunk.

So he needed home. Brandy. Thinking time. Bed.

He wasn't sure, then, why he left his motorbike where it was and walked to Sunshine's apartment block.

She would be asleep, he told himself as he reached the glass doors of the entrance. But his finger was on the apartment's intercom anyway.

'Hello?'

Her voice was not sleepy. And he remembered, then, that she worked mostly at night.

'It's Leo.'

Pause. Then buzz, click, open.

She was waiting at her door. Barefoot. In a kimono. Seriously, did this woman not own a pair of jeans or some track pants? Who slummed around alone in their own home after midnight looking like an advertisement for *Vogue* magazine in a purple kimono complete with a bloody *obi*?

Her hair was loose, her face pale, her eyes strained.

He was going to thank her for saving Rob's life.

He was going to ask her why she knew how to do the Heimlich manoeuvre.

He was going to tell her that he'd found out exactly what had happened and that he was an idiot for thinking, when he'd seen her near Natalie, that—

She cleared her throat. 'I didn't talk to Natalie except to tell her to move out of the way.'

'I don't care about Natalie,' he said—and realised that he really, *really* didn't.

'Then why are you here?'

'I'm claiming assignation number two,' he said, and kissed her.

CHAPTER SIX

SUNSHINE DREW HIM backwards into the apartment. Kiss unbroken.

Leo slammed the door with his heel. Kiss unbroken.

Sex—just sex, Sunshine said to herself.

Leo pulled back as though she'd voiced the thought, looking at her with eyes smouldering like a hungry lion's.

Sunshine grabbed his hand and dragged him to the bedroom. Kissed him again as she flipped the light switch and the fairy's lair lights she'd had embedded in the ceiling winked to life.

He angled her so he could kiss her harder, *harder*. He started to shake—she could feel it—and he broke the kiss, his breathing ragged. He rested his cheek on the top of her head as he held her in his arms, his freight train heartbeat beneath her ear.

She heard him laugh softly and pulled back, watching as he took in the room.

It was pink. Every shade of pink from pale petal, to vibrant sari, to raspberry. The walls were the colour of cherry blossoms, stencilled in white in a riot of floral shapes and curlicues—like an extended henna tattoo. There was a chaise-longue, footstools, a window seat curtained off with diaphanous drapes. At one end of the room was a half-wall that divided the bedroom from the dressing room, with its orderly arrangement of garments, shoes, and bags, which in turn led through to her bathroom.

A scene was painted on the dividing wall: a woman donning a flowing deep rose robe. Sunshine had made it a 3D work of art, building an actual Louis XIV gilded dressing table and mirror into the scene.

There was *a lot* to look at.

Leo moved towards the bed, which was king-sized, shrouded by fuchsia hangings and piled high with cushions in macaroon pastels. He touched the gauzy curtains.

'Seriously, Sunshine?' he asked, a smile in his voice.

Sunshine arched an eyebrow. 'If you want to get laid tonight, I suggest you keep a civil tongue in your head.'

'That's not where my tongue wants to be.'

Those words made her toes curl.

'Come here, let me undress you, and we'll find some place to put it,' Leo said softly.

Sunshine walked over to him, her heart jumping.

His hands reached for the *obi*.

'Wait,' she said. 'I need to warn you—I'm…scarred.'

He waited, hands at her waist.

'The accident. I have a…a scar. Two, actually. Not…small.' She hunched a shoulder, suddenly self-conscious. 'I don't want you to be shocked.'

His response was to slowly, slowly unwrap the *obi* from around her waist, then the under-sash. The kimono fell open and Leo sucked in an audible breath.

'My God,' he said, in a voice just above a raspy whisper.

'I know—they're awful.'

Leo's fingers reached, traced along the incision marks. He shook his head. 'The *My God* wasn't about the scars, Sunshine.'

Sunshine was having trouble catching a thought, her breath. 'Then…what?'

'*My God*, you are so beautiful. And *my God*, I am itching to put my hands all over you.'

'Then do it,' she whispered. 'I have no intention of stopping you.'

His fingers tensed against her flesh. And then, with both hands, he reached for her shoulders, sliding his hands under the kimono, pushing it back until the heavy fabric dropped with a quiet whoosh to the floor. He stood gazing at her.

Sunshine kept absolutely still, watching him as his nostrils flared, his hands fisted at his sides. It was both torture and delight to stand motionless as lust shimmered between them. Leo was still fully clothed, and that somehow made her feel more wanton, sexier. Her nipples were hardened points; she could feel them throbbing. Could feel a swelling between her legs as his gaze moved over her. Down, up, down. The suspense was almost unbearable. And yet she wanted the delay. Wanted to draw things out. Slow everything down so that she could wallow in this overwhelming need caused by nothing more than his eyes on her.

Then both his hands moved. With the tips of his trembling fingers he touched the centre of her forehead. Slowly his fingers moved to the bridge of her nose, across her eyebrows, down her cheeks to her mouth, her jaw, neck, collarbones. When he got to her breasts he paused at her nipples to circle and pinch. Her knees almost buckled. But inexorably his hands moved again, fingers sliding across the long, straight scar that ran over her ribs, down to her hips, across her belly, then to the juncture of her thighs.

He stopped there. Looked intently at her bare mound, licked his lips. 'Very, very pretty,' he said.

Both hands slid between her legs, fingers playing there while her breathing quickened.

'I think we've found a place for my tongue,' he said,

suddenly finding that one excruciatingly sensitive nub, focusing there.

'Are you going to take off your clothes?' Sunshine asked breathily as his fingers continued to tease her.

'Yes. But first...'

His fingers shifted, exploring her, dipping and sliding and slipping, but always returning to that one tiny place. Sunshine gasped again. Her legs were trembling as he continued to work her, pinching, stroking, rolling, lunging into her.

'Ah, Leo— God!' Sunshine cried out, and came suddenly, with a long groan.

Her head dropped back as his fingers continued to caress her, soothing now, and then one hand cupped her possessively, stilled.

Easing away from her, he started removing his clothes with short, efficient movements. The leather jacket was shrugged off and dropped to the floor. Sweater and then T-shirt were ripped over his head. Boots were yanked off. Jeans shoved down, kicked aside.

Good Lord. He was...divine. Not a steroid-pumped muscle in his whole body. Just perfectly defined, hard, lean lines of strength. Broad shoulders. Beautifully crafted biceps. Smooth, hairless, sculpted torso with that wonderful V leading to his groin. Narrow hips. Long legs. And the jut of him, big and hard, rising from that gorgeous dark blond nest, was mouth-watering. She wanted her mouth there. And her hands. And the inside of her.

'Come here,' he said. 'I want to feel you all over me.'

Sunshine thought she might swoon, just hearing the words—except that she was desperate to take him up on that offer. She *wanted* to be all over him.

She walked into his open arms and they closed around her. The top of her head didn't even reach his chin, and the feeling of being cocooned, surrounded by him, was glorious.

'You feel good there.'

'I feel *very* good,' she said throatily, and he laughed. 'And so do you,' she added as his erection nudged her belly. 'We can get that part of you a little closer, I think.'

'No rush tonight,' he said. 'If we only have three assignations left I'm going to make them count. So...now I'd like to see you spread out on that Taj Mahal bed.'

He edged her backwards, reaching out to push the hangings aside, following her down onto the bed, kissing her as he lay on top of her.

For one fraught moment he slid between her thighs, held still, teasing both of them with the promise of the length of him as it pulsed there against her wet opening. He buried his face against her neck and sucked in a breath, another, one more.

'God, it's hard to wait,' he groaned against her hair.

'Then don't,' Sunshine said, shifting to try and get him to slip inside.

He withdrew. 'I want to play with you for a while first. And this time we won't forget the condom.'

With great concentration he arranged Sunshine on the bed against the cushions, raising her arms above her head so that her breasts were tightened and jutting, the chain she always wore caught between them.

He kissed her eyelids closed and then put his mouth at the corner of hers, his tongue flicking out to taste. She gasped, and his tongue slid smoothly inside her mouth, swirled once, then retreated to lick at the corner again. He kissed down her chin, her throat, then...nothing.

She opened her eyes to find him sitting back on his heels, looking at her. 'What's wrong?' she asked.

'Nothing,' he said. 'I just like looking at you. I don't think I've ever seen skin as pale as yours. And these...' His hands reached out, hovered over her breasts. 'I'm almost scared to touch in case I come in three seconds.'

'I want you to come.'

'No—don't move your arms,' Leo ordered, and his hands settled on her breasts, squeezed gently, massaged. 'God. God, God, God…' he said, and it really did sound like a prayer.

He lowered his head and closed his lips over one nipple, sucked it sharply so that she moaned.

He stopped instantly. 'Sorry—but you're driving me crazy. Did I hurt you?'

'No,' she said, her legs moving restlessly. 'I just want you so much. *So much,*' she wailed as his mouth sucked hard again.

He commenced a steady rhythm, tugging, tonguing, pulling back to lick.

When he shifted to the other breast she couldn't help herself—her arms came down to circle him, to pull him closer, closer.

'Come inside me,' she whispered. 'Please, Leo.'

He shook his head and started moving lower. He stopped again as his mouth touched the scar. He pulled back to see it, then touched it gently with his fingers, running them over the length of it, then across the dissecting scar that ran perpendicular to it, across her ribs towards her back.

Sunshine held her breath, waiting for…what? She didn't know. Didn't want to believe that it mattered, what he thought of her imperfections. All that mattered—all that *could* matter—was the promise of the orgasm flickering low in her belly.

And yet she didn't release her breath until he moved again, kissing his way to her mound. He stopped again. Shuddered out a breath against her. Then he was kissing her there, over and over again.

'Beautiful. Delicious,' he murmured in between licking kisses, his tongue dipping just low enough to make her squirm. 'Open wider for me.'

She shifted her legs, hips rising off the bed, soundlessly urging him to shift, to slide that clever mouth right between her spread legs. When, finally, he did, using the very tip of his tongue to separate the lips of her sex, breathing deeply as he slid the flat of his tongue along the seam, she screamed his name and climaxed almost violently.

He kept his mouth there, his tongue on that fizzing knot of nerves, until the waves receded.

And then, with a groan, he slid back up her body and thrust inside her. 'Ah, thank you, God,' he groaned, and any semblance of control snapped.

He pounded into her, teeth gritted, gripping her hips as though his life depended on leveraging himself off them so he could go harder, deeper.

Sunshine could feel his orgasm building and tightened her inner muscles, holding, wanting… 'Come, come,' she said, and then the explosion ripped through him.

Long moments later he rolled onto his back, bringing Sunshine with him so that she was lying on top, her thighs falling either side of him. 'Forgot the condom again,' he said.

Sunshine frowned. 'I've never forgotten before.'

'Do we need to talk about it?'

'Only if you have a disease.'

'Then we don't need to talk.' He secured her more tightly against his chest. One hand was in her hair, smoothing through the strands.

Silence. Minutes dragged on.

Then, 'The Heimlich thing… Why?' he asked.

She shrugged, self-conscious. 'I saw a story on the internet about a woman who choked to death. If someone had known what to do she wouldn't have died. So I…I learned.

Just in case. Typical that the first time I had to use it was on Natalie's boyfriend!'

'He's not her boyfriend. He's her bitch.'

'Ouch.'

'I wish I could say that was me being malicious, but it's just the truth.'

'I certainly don't understand what you saw in her.'

'Me neither. I guess we get what we deserve.'

She looked up at him, perplexed. 'Why would you think you deserved her? Deserved...*that*?'

Leo shook his head, shrugged, clearly uncomfortable. 'Just history. Perpetuating the crappiness of my life. Because she wasn't my first mistake—just the most persistent.'

Mistake. Something about the word made Sunshine shiver. Mistake...

'You're cold,' Leo said. 'And I have a brilliant idea— let's actually get *in* the bed.'

Sunshine latched onto being cold as a viable excuse for the sudden chill prickling along her skin. She slid under the covers, busied herself positioning cushions so that she was propped up against the bedhead, half turned to him.

She toyed with her chain, rubbing the sun and moon charms between her fingers.

'Sun and moon,' Leo said, watching her. 'For Sunshine and Moonbeam?'

'Yes. The business is called Sun & Moon too. Not sure what we were going to do when we changed our names.'

'You were going to change your names? Don't tell me: Sue and Jenny?'

'Do I look like a Sue?'

'Actually, you look like a Sunshine.'

'Harsh! Well, Moonbeam was definitely *not* a Jenny! She was going to be Amaya—it means Night Rain. She figured it was a close enough association with the night, if not with the moon specifically.'

'Nice. And yours?'

'Allyn. Do I look like an Allyn?'

'I told you—you look like a Sunshine.'

'Oh, dear. Daunting. Well, Moon said Allyn meant Bright and Shining One. Close enough to sunshine, in her opinion. And she said it suited me.' She frowned, thinking. 'I've thought a lot over the past two years about making the change. Wondered if doing the thing we planned to do together on my own would help me accept...move on. My parents aren't so sure.'

'Tell me about them,' Leo said.

'My parents? Oh, they're very zen! Quite mad. And completely wonderful. Always there. Supportive, but never smothering. They let Moon and me leave the commune when we were fifteen, so we could see a different way and make informed decisions about how we wanted to live. They made sure we had a safe place to stay, a good school to go to, money for whatever we needed, while we worked it out. And they seemed to understand even before we did that Moon was the true hippie and I was... well, something in between a hippie and an urbanite. Moon would have raced straight back to the commune if not for me being anchored in the city.' She smiled, remembering. 'We started our business with money our father inherited but didn't need. It was given to us simply, with love, on our eighteenth birthday.'

'Lucky.'

'Yes. But it's not all sparkles and roses, you know. There's the haiku to deal with!'

'Ah, the haiku. What is it?'

'You'll find out—that poem is coming.'

'Can't wait.'

'You have no idea!'

'But…they were okay with you girls changing your names?'

'They weren't insulted, if that's what you mean. They were fine with it if we wanted to do it.' She bit her lip. 'But Dad had a sidebar conversation with me because he thought Moonbeam was browbeating me.'

'And was she?'

'Not browbeating—nothing that brutish. She was… *persuading*!' Sunshine said, and smiled, remembering. 'But I was happy enough to be persuaded if she wanted it that badly. And I owed her, for staying.'

Sunshine closed her eyes, picturing her sister.

'Tell me more about Moonbeam,' Leo said.

Opening her eyes on a sigh, Sunshine adjusted her position in the bed. 'Well, you know what she looked like—me! But slimmer. And with the most beautiful green eyes— both of them. Other than looks, though, we were completely different. I was the carnivore; she was vegetarian. I was…well, as you see me. Friendly, touchy-feely, chirpy.'

'And…?'

Sunshine fiddled with her necklace. 'Moon was… intriguing. I was *Mary Poppins*; she was *Crouching Tiger, Hidden Dragon*. When the kids made fun of my devil eyes I would laugh it off, but she would go all superhero.' She laughed suddenly. '*Is* there a hippie superhero? What a wonderful idea. I'm going to do a web search on that.'

'So she was your protector?'

'Oh, yes. And my cheer squad. And my…everything. She was smart, and had an amazing flair for numbers, so although the business was my idea she was the CEO. And she didn't even want to be in the city!'

Sunshine adjusted the quilt. Fussed with a cushion.

'She said that left me to concentrate on the creative stuff because she was not into fashion like I was. She would wear a suit for business if I chose it for her; otherwise she would drag on whatever clothes and shoes came to hand. I, on the other hand, was obsessed with colour and shape and style.' She shrugged, a little sheepish. 'And I really love shoes!'

'Funny, I hadn't noticed that.'

She hit him with the cushion. 'Don't make me take you behind that wall and show you my shoe collection. I haven't known a man yet who could cope with the sight.'

'Are you *really* going there? Talking about the men you've had in here? I'll go there if you want, Sunshine, but I don't think you'll like it.'

She opened her eyes at him. 'Oh, that sounds very alpha male.'

He didn't smile. 'You'll see alpha, beta, gamma, *and* zeta male if you go near another man, Sunshine.'

'Oh, alpha, beta, *and* zeta?'

'Alpha-beta-*gamma*-zeta. And don't roll your eyes.'

'Sorry.'

'I said don't roll your eyes.'

'All *right*!' Sunshine said, laughing.

'So, I think,' Leo said quietly, after a long moment, 'we're up to the bike, aren't we?'

Sunshine nodded, sat a little straighter. 'The bike,' she said. She pulled a different cushion onto her lap and started playing with the fringe. 'She bought it because she liked the wind in her face and the freedom of riding. It was too big for her, but she wouldn't be told.'

She stopped there.

'And...?' he prompted.

Sunshine reached for the charms. 'We were at a party. Her boyfriend *du jour*—Jeff—mixed us up and tried to kiss me. Moonbeam went into melodrama mode and stormed off, dragging me with her.'

'Was she angry with you?'

'God, no! She knew I would never poach. And truthfully…? She wasn't even angry with Jeff. She was just restless. Bored with being in the city. And tired of Jeff. So what he did gave her an excuse to dump him. She thought…she thought he'd done it accidentally-on-purpose because he actually preferred me. We were dressed so differently, you see, it couldn't have been a mix-up.'

'Did that happen often? A boyfriend switching sides?'

'No. Never before.'

'And so…?'

'And so we clambered onto the bike.' She shivered. 'She was wild that night, riding too fast. She took a turn badly, and…well. Moonbeam died instantly. Her neck snapped at the base of the helmet.' She swallowed. 'I got carted off to hospital, where I went through twenty-eight pints of blood.' She moved restlessly. 'Internal bleeding. They had to take my spleen—which apparently you don't really need, so go figure! And they took half my liver, which was haemorrhaging. Actually, did you know that the liver regenerates? Which means the chunk of my liver they cut out has probably grown back. Amazing!'

'I'm sorry, Sunshine,' Leo said.

She rearranged herself in the bed again—flustery, unnecessary activity. 'Which brings us to the important part of this discussion. Getting rid of your motorbike.'

Leo said nothing.

'Leo? You understand, don't you?'

He nodded slowly. 'I understand why you hate motorbikes—because you blame yourself for the accident. You feel guilty because you couldn't talk your sister out of that bike. Because she stayed in the city only for you, where she was an unhappy fish out of water. Because of what her boyfriend did. The way all those things led to both of you being on the bike at that precise moment at that speed. Because she died and you didn't. And you're here and she's not.'

Sunshine brushed away a tear. 'That's about the sum of it. I just miss her so much. And I'd do anything to have her back.' She looked at him. 'But you can't bring someone back from the dead. So *please* get rid of it, Leo. Please?'

'You don't understand what that bike means to me.' He grimaced. 'My parents…they were druggies, and they didn't give a damn. Your parents made sure you had support. I was my own support—and Caleb's. Your parents made sure you had money, but when I was still a child I had to steal it, beg it, or make it—and I did all three! There was never food on the table unless I put it there. So I haunted restaurants around the city, pleading for leftovers. Eventually one of the chefs took pity on me and I got a job in a kitchen, and…' Shrug. 'Here I am.'

Sunshine touched his hand.

He looked at where her hand was, on his, with an odd expression on his face. And then he drew his hand away.

'I'm not telling you all that to get sympathy, just to explain,' he said. 'And it could have been a lot worse. We weren't sexually abused. Or beaten—well, not Caleb. And me not often, or more than I could take. Mainly we were just not important. Like a giant mistake that you can't fix so you try to forget it. I grew up fast and hard—I had to. The upshot is that I don't do frivolity. I'm not sociable unless there's something in it for me. I don't stop to smell the roses and hug the trees. I just push on, without indulging myself. Except for my bike.'

'I see,' Sunshine said. And she did. It was so very simple. Leo had his bike the way she had Moon's ashes. Something that connected you to what you'd lost—what you couldn't have: in her case her sister; in his a carefree youth.

She swallowed around a sudden lump. 'We're not going to find common ground on this, are we? Because you deserve one piece of youthful folly and I can't bear what that piece happens to be.'

She got out of bed, grabbed her kimono off the floor, quickly pulled it on, and turned to face him. 'This means, of course, that we'll have to call it quits at two.'

'At two…what? O'clock?'

'Two *times*—as in not *four*. As in assignations.'

'Why?'

Why? She had a sudden memory of that electri-fried bat. 'Because the thought of you on that bike already upsets me too much. That's going to get harder, not easier, to cope with if we keep doing…*this*.'

'This?'

'Sex,' she said impatiently. 'It's my fault for starting it, and I'll cop to that. I threw myself at you when you didn't want to go there. The blame is squarely here, with me.'

'If we're talking blame, I threw myself at you tonight.'

Sunshine dragged the edges of the kimono closed and started looking around for her sash. 'Well, let's *un*throw ourselves.'

'Come back to bed, Sunshine, and we'll talk about it.'

'Bed is the wrong place to talk.'

'Four assignations was what we agreed on,' Leo said.

'*Up to!* They're the salient words. *Up to* four. I've never got to four before. I've never got past two! And you can see why. It gets too emotional.'

Leo shoved the quilt aside, got out of bed. 'I'll do you a deal on the motorbike,' he offered, and started tugging on his clothes.

'What kind of deal?'

Wary. *Very* wary.

'I'll get rid of the bike the day after our fourth assignation. Or when you change your name to Allyn. Whichever comes first.'

She licked her lips nervously. 'That's an odd deal.'

'Is it? I'm offering to give up a piece of a past I never really had—the bike. In return, you give up something you can't accept is past its use-by date—your sister's two-year hold over you.'

'She doesn't have a hold over me.'

'If she didn't have a hold over you the four times thing wouldn't exist. So—my bike for going where no man has gone before and risking the magic number four.'

'No.'

'Then take the alternative option and change your name. You said it might be a way of moving on, so do it. Move on, Sunshine, one way or the other.'

'I...I don't know,' she said, agonised.

'Take some time and think about it,' he said. 'But not too long. Because—in case you haven't quite figured me out yet—I don't wait for what I want. I just go out and get it. Even if I have to steal it.'

'You don't really want me.'

'I'm like an immortal lobster—who really knows? Let's get to number four and see.'

'Well, you can't *steal me.*'

'Don't bet on it, sweetheart. I've spent my life getting my own way. And I can take things from you that you never knew you had.'

She located her *obi* and whipped it up off the floor. 'That's not even worth a response.'

Leo just smiled and started pulling on his boots.

She tried, twice, to tie the sash, but her fingers were clumsy.

And Leo's hands were suddenly there—capable, efficient, tying it easily.

'Thank you,' she said stiffly when he had finished, and flicked her hair over her shoulders. 'I'll see you out.'

She walked Leo to the apartment door. 'So!' she said. 'I'll email you about...about the clothes for the wedding and a few other things. And then... Well...'

'And then...well...?' Leo repeated, looking a little too

wolfish and a lot too jaunty for a man who was waiting for an answer about sex that could, should—no, *would*!—go against him. And then he leant down and kissed her quickly on the mouth.

She jumped back as though he'd scalded her.

'It's just a *stolen* kiss, Sunshine,' he murmured. 'Think of the calories.'

Sunshine stared into the darkness long after returning to bed.

Leo would give up his motorbike.

Into her head popped an image of Moonbeam—laughing as they left the party that night. Giving a wild shout as she started the bike. Zooming off with Sunshine on the back, gripping her tightly.

And then darkness. And that feeling. Waking up in hospital and knowing, without needing to be told, that Moonbeam was gone. She never wanted to experience that desolating ache again.

Leo didn't understand what it would do to her if something happened to him. And that said it all, didn't it? She'd only known him for one week, and already she was terrified that something would happen to him.

What a conundrum. She could get him to give up his bike if she slept with him twice more. But if she slept with him twice more she would be getting dangerously close to him. And she couldn't risk that.

Or...

She could get him to give up his bike if she changed her name. And she just wasn't sure what that would mean. Maybe it would help her accept Moon's death. But maybe it would be a betrayal—taking a twins' decision and making it a solo decision. Moving on when Moon couldn't.

And did anything matter more than keeping Leo safe?

Sunshine threw off the covers—what a restless night

this was turning out to be!—and yanked on her kimono, leaving it fluttering as she raced from the room and into her office.

There, on the high-gloss blue bureau, was her sister. Her sister, who had wanted her ashes to be scattered at a beach under a full moon.

Instead here she was. Beautifully housed in a stunning antique cloisonné urn featuring all the colours of the rainbow.

But an urn—no matter how beautiful—wasn't the ocean.

And the ocean was where Moonbeam belonged.

Leo stared into the darkness, thinking about the simple pleasure of touch.

It didn't take a psychologist to work out what his issue was—the fact that his parents had never touched him the way other parents touched their children. Because there had been more important things to do than give their son the affection he craved. Like shoot up. Suck in the crack. Snort up the meth.

It had been different for Caleb, because Leo had made it so. Leo had looked after Caleb, put his needs first, fought his battles, protected him. And so Caleb wasn't reserved, wary, driven, and damaged—like Leo. Caleb attracted affection and gentleness and love. Leo attracted people like Natalie, for whom his remoteness was a challenge and his celebrity something to use.

'You're choosing wrong,' Sunshine had said—but what if he was choosing *right* and he was getting exactly what he deserved?

It wasn't as if he could choose Sunshine Smart as an alternative. She didn't *want* to be chosen by anyone.

So why he was offering to give up his motorbike for her was a mystery.

So what if he never had sex with her again?

So what if she went on grieving for her sister for the rest of the life?

Leo punched his pillow. Forced his eyes closed.

And there she was, warning him about her scars. So beautiful. And damaged, like him. But wanting to *stay* damaged—*unlike* him.

His eyes popped open and he punched the pillow again.

God, but she irked him.

Her perkiness irked him. Partly because he wanted to think that it made her shallow...and yet she'd learned the Heimlich manoeuvre and wasn't afraid to use it.

The way she chucked crazy facts into her arguments—about the sexual habits of praying mantises, the questionable immortality of lobsters, regenerating livers, and so on and on and on—irked him. Because most of the time that stuff was fascinating. And even if it wasn't, it was fascinating to watch those unique eyes glow with the wonder of it.

Her boring living room irked him, because it shouldn't be like that. Not that her décor was any of his business. And the fact that he could be bothered to think of her apartment irking him irked him too.

Her pink bedroom irked him. All right, it didn't—because it was kind of amazing. But it *should* irk him, and the fact that it *didn't* irk him irked him.

Her propensity to kiss and touch and pet him irked him. And it had irked him even more when she hadn't kissed him hello at the restaurant.

Her four-times maximum irked him. And the fact that he'd refused to accept that they were stopping at two irked him.

Two times. *Two.* Not three, not four—two! Her terms. Everything on her terms, right from the moment she'd ambushed him on the couch.

Well, he'd picked her as a wily little dictator from Day One. But she was *not* going to dictate to Leo Quartermaine. He would have her as many damned times as he *wanted* to have her.

He punched his pillow again. Hard.

CHAPTER SEVEN

TO: Leo Quartermaine
FROM: Sunshine Smart
SUBJECT: Wedding update
Hi Leo

I'm attaching a photo of my dress. If you can send me one of your suit and tie—I'm assuming a tie?—I'll know if this is okay or if I have to go back to the drawing board. And I can get your shoe design finished too.

So, the shoes. You'll need three fittings—twenty mins each time—and you can schedule these to suit yourself as I won't be needed. I'm attaching Seb's business card— Seb is the shoemaker—and once you've approved my design all you need to do is call him.

And, trust me, once you've had custom-made shoes you'll never go back. Which might not be good, now I think of it, because they're hellishly expensive (not these particular shoes, of course, because it's a special deal for me, as well as being a present).

The other attachment is of some floral arrangements for the restaurant. I think the all-white ones, so as not to distract from the view. What do you think?

I'm going to scoot down the coast on Sunday to check out some hotel options for guests who want to stay overnight. I know you're super-busy so I can handle this and email all the info to you.

And then we need to confirm the music—Kate is amazing—when you have a minute.

Hope all is well.

Sunshine

Oh, no, Sunshine Smart-Ass, you are not going down the coast without me.

That was the first thought to leap to Leo's mind after he read the email.

The second was that she had a bloody nerve adding the 'Hope all is well', because she had to know all was *not* well. Not by a country *mile* was all 'well'. 'All' wouldn't be 'well' until he had her exactly where he wanted her.

A sudden image of her naked, in his arms, had him erect and almost groaning. Even though that was not what he'd meant. What he'd meant was on her knees and—

Argh. Another image.

Figuratively speaking on her knees, not physically.

But—nope, the image wouldn't budge.

He took a steadying breath and forced himself to open Sunshine's attachment, hoping it wouldn't be her *in* the damned dress—which, of course, it was. Looking very hot. And, of course, she had her foot stuck out so he could see her amazingly sexy shoes.

And, since he knew he had to see her in the flesh in that dress, he would up the ante on his suit so that he matched the formality—*and* send her the damned photo so he could get his shoe design.

And he would tell her that he would most definitely meet her at South on Sunday, when they would discuss flowers and confirm music and go and see the hotels *together*.

Ha!

Hope all is well.

Bloody, *bloody* nerve.

* * *

Sunshine, who had laboured long and hard over the wording of her email to Leo to give it just the right sense of moving-on friendliness, opened Leo's reply with some trepidation.

She wasn't sure what to expect—but the three terse lines certainly hadn't been laboured over.

Meet you at South at two p.m. Sunday. Will confirm everything then. Suit pic attached.

So! She guessed she'd better start working on getting rid of the horrible fluttery feeling in her stomach before Sunday. *Surely* she could be her normal carefree self in four days!

Cautiously she opened the attachment he'd sent.

And—oh—flutter, flutter, flutter. And he wasn't even *in* the photo!

The suit, photographed on a dummy so she got the full effect, was in a beautiful mid-grey. Three pieces, including a waistcoat, which she adored. The pants were narrow and cuffed. The two-button jacket was ultra-contemporary, but also sexily conservative. A white shirt, a tie in a fine black, silver and white check, and a purple and silver pocket square shoved insouciantly into the left breast pocket.

That suit, his physique, his dourly handsome face, his hair... He would have all the female guests drooling over him.

Maybe she shouldn't have made him grow his hair... *And where did* that *unworthy thought come from? If three centimetres of hair snares him a new bed partner—good!*

Well, every woman might be drooling, but only one woman could design his shoes. All right, that sounded incredibly lame. But so what?

She was going to do the design right now. And give it

to him on Sunday. And he was going to love—not like, but *love*—his shoes, dammit!

The motorbike was in pole position when Sunshine pulled up outside South. He couldn't have made it more visible if he'd had it on a dais under a spotlight.

She knew right then that he would be yanking her chain all day. *Stealing* her sanity!

Her stomach, which had finally started to settle into a relatively stable buzz, started rioting again. She sat in her car, taking some deep breaths and giving herself a stern talking-to: he was not a teenage hothead and he would *not* kill himself; she didn't care if he *did* kill himself; *she'd* kill him if he didn't get rid of the bike. And so on.

Not the most intelligent conversation she'd ever had with herself. And completely ineffectual, because her stomach was still going crazy.

If *only* she'd had the nous to call it quits with Leo after the first time she might still be a properly functioning adult.

Well, spilt milk and all that. She would just have to find a way back to normality before it affected the wedding preparations. Because the wedding was what was important. Not her, not Leo—the wedding!

She straightened her shoulders, flung open the door, and scrambled out of the car. She would have liked to have *disembarked* from the car, in case Leo was watching, but she was wearing her most complicated shoes and a too-tight dress! Compensating, she practically glided to the boot and, with what she considered great panache, swung her portfolio out. She left the briefcase behind, though—it was hard to look cucumber-cool when you were carrying a briefcase *and* a portfolio. Not that it usually bothered her, but... Well, *but*!

She took another deep breath as she entered the restaurant and saw Leo.

His hair was at Number Three buzz-cut stage. His jeans were black. He was wearing a fitted black superfine wool sweater. Sex on a stick. Even the black biker boots didn't have the power to dampen the desire that hit her like a punch.

He walked towards her—a purposeful kind of prowl that made her tongue want to loll. *Not* that there would be any tongue-lolling going on today.

She went to give him a reflex kiss on the cheek, but pulled back as it hit her that this was now fraught with difficulty.

His slow smile told her he'd registered her state of confusion. And then, to her shock, he leant down and kissed *her*. Sweet, slow, warm brush of lips against her cheek.

'Oh,' she said inanely.

He simply raised his eyebrows. And she knew what he was doing. He was playing the *Dare You* game! *Dare you to question that.* Well, she would *not* be dared.

He gestured to the dining area. 'As you can see, the tables and chairs are in,' he said. 'We're basically ready. I'm doing a trial dinner in two weeks, then we'll have a month to tweak. It will be a full moon on the trial night, so the view should be amazing. I'm inviting mostly locals, and some food and lifestyle media, but because it's a rehearsal for the wedding you'll have to come—obviously.'

Dare you! Dare you not to come.

Oh, how she wanted to say she couldn't make it. But that would be a mammoth case of cutting off her nose to spite her face, which he knew very well.

So, 'Of course,' she said.

He nodded at the portfolio in her hand. 'What's that?'

'Your shoe design.'

'Let's have a look,' Leo said.

Ordinarily, Sunshine would have gone a little theatrical, starting with a narrative and then positioning the designs on an easel. But today she merely pulled out the sheets and thrust them at Leo.

She watched, trying not to care, as he flicked through them.

She saw the shock come over his face and wished she could snatch the drawings out of his hands and rip them up.

Leo took them further into the restaurant and laid the pages on a window table, where light streamed brightly through.

He darted a looked up at her. 'Not what I was expecting,' he said.

'What *were* you expecting?'

Small pause. Quick smile. 'What's the shoe equivalent of a pine bookshelf?'

Huh? 'I guess…black leather lace-ups…?'

'Bingo.'

'Not that there's anything wrong with black leather lace-ups.'

'And yet…?'

Sunshine shrugged. 'And…yet.'

Okay. Leo admitted it. He wanted the damned shoes.

The design was sharp, lean, streamlined. No decorative stitching. Toes that were subtly rounded but also somehow pointed. No laces—monkstraps, fastened with sleek silver side buckles.

Plain and yet edgy.

And the colour was astounding. They looked black, but there was a suggestion…a sheen…of purple.

He cleared his throat. 'Thanks.'

'Do you…do you think you'll wear them?'

'Can you really get that colour? And those buckles?'

'I have the black-violet leather reserved. And I've already ordered the buckles—they're real silver.'

Black-violet. Perfect. 'Then, yes, I'll wear them, Sunshine.'

She smiled, her eyes glowing with joy, and he felt his heart start that heavy thump he'd hoped wouldn't happen. Not today—not when he wanted to be securely in the driver's seat for a change, keeping Sunshine a little off balance.

Of course his first sight of her, hauling herself out of that ancient, minuscule bright yellow car—Holy Mother of God, could a car *be* more perfect for her?—had almost derailed that plan on the spot, because *he* was the one who'd felt suddenly off balance.

It was the dress, he told himself. It was a monumental distraction, that dress. Petal-pink, too damned tight, too damned short.

And the black heels—too bloody high, with little black pearls studded in the leather and those crisscrossed ribbons around her ankles. How could a man *not* think about sucking her toes when he saw those shoes?

Thank God he'd got that first surge of heat under control enough to kiss her cheek instead of shoving his tongue halfway down her throat. Because that had been touch and go!

Now, however, the heart-thump suggested derailment was imminent again.

Well, he would just have to share the derailment around.

'So, then, let's go check out hotels,' he said.

'Are you—? Are you going to come with me? In the car?'

He thought about saying no—he'd realised that seeing him on the bike was going to be her breaking point and he wanted to get to that point fast. But in that tiny car of hers they would be very close to each other. So close she'd be able to feel him even without touching. He could use that. He was *sure* he could use that.

'Yes,' he said. 'The car.'

But when he squeezed himself into the passenger seat, and the scent of jonquils hit him like Thor's hammer, he thought perhaps he had made a tactical error. He just freaking *loved* that smell.

'Seat belt,' she said, and waited like a good little Girl Scout until he'd buckled up before starting the car.

He could see a faint blush on her cheeks. She'd get a shock if he touched her there. One finger along the rosy heat.

So he did, finding it shockingly easy to do.

But touchy-feely Sunshine swivelled as though he'd slapped her.

She stared at him.

He stared back.

And then he smiled. 'You know, Sunshine—your pupils are dilated. Got any internet facts to share about dilated pupils?'

Yes, Sunshine knew all about dilated pupils.

But she wasn't answering that.

Not with visions of straddling him right there in his seat popping into her head. He was so close that every time she changed gears her hand brushed his thigh. She had a sneaking suspicion he was deliberately putting his leg in the way. Another yank of her chain? She'd said hands-off, so he—the great un-toucher—had decided it was hands-*on*, just to needle her into a decision. And she'd thought he'd needed exposure therapy for his touching phobia!

It was just as well the first hotel was close to the restaurant. It was such a relief to be out of the car and in the open air.

Until Leo put his hand in the small of her back to guide

her across the car park to the hotel entrance—*enough with the touching, already!*—and she wanted to slap him.

She was a *pacifist*—she should *not* want to slap!

Sunshine stepped away from Leo the moment they were inside the hotel.

'I loved what I saw on the internet about this place,' she said, with an enthusiasm that actually managed to sound insincere even though she truly meant it.

That was what Leo was doing to her. Making her over-babble.

She looked around, taking in the use of dark wood, the pale stone floor. 'I think I'm going to book my own room here. Are you planning on staying overnight? I think you should. You know, you don't want to…to ride…after the party.'

Babbling. Shut up, shut up!

'I won't be riding home if I don't have a bike,' he pointed out calmly. Yanking her goddamned chain! 'But in any case I have a house here, and hopefully there'll be furniture by then.'

'A house? By then?'

Ugh. She'd turned into a parrot. A babbling parrot.

'The house was only built last year, and it's largely a furniture-free zone.'

'Are you going to live down here permanently?'

'Not permanently. I have too much on my plate in Sydney.'

Sunshine knew all about having too much on your plate. It kept you nicely occupied so you only had to think, not feel.

Think. Not feel.

That sounded good.

Think, not feel.

If she just remembered that everything would be all right.

And if she thought—ha—*thought!*—about Leo's full
plate, it was clear that although he might talk about this
mythical abyss-jumping woman of his dreams he was no
different from her. He couldn't *fit* that kind of commit-
ment into his life. Otherwise he would have it by now.
He had enough women to choose from, for God's sake!
She'd looked him up on the internet again yesterday, and
seen the paparazzi photos. And, all right, that particular
bit of searching had been a weak moment that she would
not be repeating!

So! He didn't have it because he didn't want it.

And neither did she.

So she could stop the silly panicking.

Think, not feel.

'You could stay with me,' Leo said as one of the hotel
staff approached them. 'The night of the reception.'

Okay, she couldn't stop panicking just yet, because her
stomach was rioting again. 'I don't think that would be a
good idea.'

'Don't have to think,' Leo said, and touched her cheek.
'You can just feel.'

How the *hell* did he lock on to her thoughts like that?
'You are freaking me out, Leo.'

'Am I?' He sounded delighted. 'All you have to do is
agree to two more times and I'll stop!'

Sunshine turned gratefully to the hotel manager.

Introductions. Small talk. All good.

And then the manager asked, 'Shall we start the tour
with the honeymoon suite?'

Sunshine choked on a laugh.

Which made Leo choke on a laugh.

So much unresolved between them—seething lust, and
different takes on life, and twisted psyches—and here they

were, being whisked off to the honeymoon suite like a couple of newlyweds.

'Wonderful,' Leo said, biting the inside of his cheek as Sunshine choked again.

She carefully kept her eyes off him when they reached the suite, looking around with a desperate kind of eagerness.

The suite had a touch of Bali about it, with a low bed of dark carved wood and a beautiful wood floor leading out to a private bamboo garden and plunge pool.

'Oh, so perfect! I might book it for myself,' Sunshine gushed.

Oh, no, you won't. 'Or for the actual honeymooners, perhaps?'

'Oops. Got carried away! Bamboo does that to me.'

'*Bamboo* does that?'

'Yes. Did you know it produces up to thirty-five per cent more oxygen than hardwood trees and absorbs four times as much carbon?'

'No, Sunshine, I did not. But I can see how that would make you want to honeymoon with it. There's something so sexy about carbon absorption.'

She giggled, then choked again as she tried to stop it. 'Well, I'm sure there are other wonderful rooms here that will suit me very well,' she said.

'I'm sure there are, but you'll like my place better,' Leo said, and almost laughed to see the flicker of panic race across her face.

Her face was flushed, her eyes wide, her lips parted so he could see that little gap between her teeth.

And, God, he wanted her. Wanted to run his hands up her legs and under her dress. To put his mouth on her, make her beg. Wanted to hear her sigh his name, feel her shudder. Wanted—

Ouch. To do something with his painful erection.

Okay—they were going to have to rush through this hotel tour.

Then rush through the next hotel.

Because it was three o'clock.

And by four o'clock he intended to have her at his house, preferably naked.

'So! Leo!' Sunshine said, pulling up at South at a quarter to four. 'Accommodation is sorted. I'll cover the card with the list of charities for donations in lieu of gifts and get that included with the invitation. Roger to no MC—just you welcoming the guests. No official speeches, just a repeat of their wedding vows. Clothes are done. Shoes underway. Kate is on board to sing. I think we can cover everything else via email.'

Leo hadn't made a move to get out of the car. He just sat there.

'Cake,' he said.

'The—the guys can just pick that, can't they? Like you originally suggested.'

'Sunshine, I brought down four miniature decorated cakes because you wanted a tasting, and if you think I'm taking them, untouched, back to Anton—who is monumentally temperamental and had to be talked into making them in the first place—you can think again.' *Forgive me, mild-mannered Anton...*

'Oh, then I guess… Or maybe I could cut a piece of each and—'

'And then there's the seating plan. I've got the night off.' *Go, Pinocchio.* 'I don't know when I'll get another, so we may as well get that sorted.'

'But I—I…I have a date.'

'Date?'

'Er…Tony. The calligrapher.'

'The calligrapher is an ex. Break the date.'

'How do you know he's an—? Oh, I told you, didn't I?'

'Yep. And in any case we haven't resolved the two versus four issue—you're mine until we do.'

Sunshine dragged in a breath. Held it.

'Breathe, Sunshine. It's just cake.' *Like hell.* 'And I also have a sample Anton made as a potential wedding favour to show you.'

She was looking torn. 'But we could do *that* via email.'

'And I have everything I need to make meat-lovers' pizza.'

Her mouth fell open. 'Oh, well, in that case.' She started getting out of the car.

'What are you doing?' Leo asked.

'Going into the restaurant.'

'No, we're going to my house.'

'I thought there wasn't any furniture.'

'It's not quite *that* basic. There's a completely fitted-out kitchen. With food. And a makeshift dining suite, although the table is on wheels. Some balcony furniture. Bathroom stuff. A mattress.'

Dare you! Dare you to come!

Her nose was wrinkling up; he could practically see the arguments bouncing around in her head.

'Think of the cake, Sunshine.'

'All right,' she said, with the air of a Christian martyr marching towards the lions' den.

'Good,' Leo said, and started getting out of the car.

'What are you doing?'

'I'll take the bike. You follow me. I'll grab my jacket and keys while you call Tony.'

'Tony?' she asked, blankly. And then, 'Oh, yes. Tony. I...'

'Forgot Tony? Poor Tony.'

For the first time ever Leo rode like a bat out of hell.

He didn't feel good about it, because he knew Sunshine

would be in a state—but he also knew it was the most effective way to smash through the wall she was trying to erect between them. The best way to *not* end up like Tony and all the others who had never got to the magical fourth assignation.

Well, Leo Quartermaine was not a piece of meat. He was getting to number four, and if it took the damned motorbike to get there so be it.

He was going so fast he had to pass the house and double back twice so Sunshine could keep sight of him. She was still lagging behind when he zoomed off the road and into the carport, but he was sure she'd been watching him closely and would find her way.

He wondered what she'd think of his place. The nondescript carport gave no hint that it was the gateway to a modern architectural masterpiece. Once they left the carport, however, and headed down a steep set of steps, it would be like entering a different world. The house was basically a long, horizontal strip of wood and glass cut into the side of a low cliff. A second set of steps led from the house to a beach so secluded it was like Leo's private patch of ocean.

The Fiat finally puttered in and Leo braced himself for her reaction, looking closely at her partly averted face as she got out of the car.

Very blank, very pale.

Without speaking to him she went to the boot, took out a cherry-red briefcase, fixed the strap over her shoulder. And then she turned towards him, and he saw that the weird face-morph thing had happened, that she was trembling.

And Leo knew he could never do that to her again.

She followed him to the top of the stairs, where he stopped. 'Are you all right?'

She merely looked at him, but he was relieved to see things settling back into place.

'Take off your shoes,' Leo said. 'It will be safer.'

'Don't talk to me about *safe*.'

'Then give me your briefcase.'

'No. Let's just see how you like thinking about my breaking body tumbling down those stairs, with my anklebones smashed in these heels and my briefcase cracking my skull open.'

'All right. I'm sorry I rode like that.'

She was speechless for a moment, and then she drew back her arm and punched him in the shoulder. At least it looked like a punch; it felt more like a slap with a cushion. 'You told me you weren't a teenage hothead,' she said shakily.

'I'm not. I'm sorry.'

'Shut up, Leo. I'm too angry with you to hear an apology. And there had better be six kinds of meat on that pizza after putting me through that! And *buffalo* mozzarella!'

Buffalo mozzarella—what a zinger.

He only barely managed not to laugh. 'Just give me the damned briefcase,' he said, biting the inside of his cheek.

She punched him again. Same shoulder. She clearly wasn't a candidate for cage fighting if that was the best she could do. 'You are *not* carrying my briefcase, Mr Alpha-Beta-Zeta,' Sunshine said.

'Don't forget the Gamma.'

She tossed her hair over her shoulder and waved him imperiously on: start the descent.

Leo took the first step, and the next, and the next, navigating slowly, staying just a half-step ahead. If Sunshine stumbled, if she even gasped, he would turn and catch her and toss her over his shoulder and carry her even if she kicked and screamed all the way.

But Sunshine—the epitome of high-heeled confidence—didn't put a foot wrong, and they arrived at the entrance to the house without incident. He opened the door and gestured her in ahead of him.

The use of glass was similar to what he'd done at South, except that where South had windows the house had full-length glass doors, opening onto a long veranda. The view was just as stunning. But because the house was so much lower, and perched within a cove, it had a more intimate connection with the beach.

Sunshine was walking slowly, uncertainly, to the glass doors.

'Go out,' Leo urged, stripping off his jacket and tossing it onto one of the few chairs.

She put down her briefcase and slid one of the doors open. Stepped onto the wooden deck, walked over to the edge.

He followed her out, wondering what was going through her head as she looked out.

'My sister would have loved this,' she said.

Moonbeam. *Quelle surprise.* 'And you?'

She half turned, looked into his eyes. He could see the tears swimming.

Because of Moonbeam? Or him and his bone-headed motorbike stunt?

Whatever! Leo simply reeled her in, held her close.

So mind-bogglingly easy to touch her now he'd set his course. So easy…

Her head was on his shoulder, and then she turned her face to kiss the shoulder she had punched earlier.

'I'm sorry for punching you,' she said. 'I've never punched anyone before.'

'I don't know how to break it to you, but those punches didn't hurt.'

'Then I hope it hurts washing my Beige Amour lipstick out of your woollen top. And I won't be sorry if it *doesn't* come out.'

'You can draw a map on the back in Beige Amour, okay? I deserve it.'

He could feel her breath, her spiky lashes against his neck.

'You made me so mad,' she said.

'I know. I'm sorry.'

'And you're supposed to have haphephobia. We shouldn't be standing like this.'

'I'm supposed to have *what*?'

'Fear of touch.'

He swallowed the laugh. This was *not* the time to make fun of her. 'But, Sunshine, we *are* standing like this. Maybe that means I'm making progress on my phobia. So…how's *your* phobia tracking?'

He heard her breath hitch, felt it catch in her chest. She pulled out of his arms and turned back to the view for a long moment. He thought she wasn't going to answer, but then she turned back.

'If you mean my reluctance to get emotionally close to people, that's not a phobia—it's an active choice.'

'The wrong choice.'

'The right choice for me.' And then she gave a shuddery kind of sound that was like a cross between a sigh and a laugh. 'Okay, you've yanked my chain. I've punched you. Let's move on before I start boring myself. We have things to do, so onwards and upwards: let them eat cake! Did you know that Marie Antoinette never actually said that?'

Sunshine took herself off to explore the house while Leo prepared the cakes.

The house was designed to give most rooms a view. There was a generous living/dining area, a cosy library, which had shelves but no books, and two private wings—the main bedroom/bathroom wing, with an atrium that reminded her of the honeymoon suite at the hotel, except that it was plant-free, and the other with three bedrooms, each with an en suite bathroom.

Leo had thrown a roll of paper towels at her when she'd poked her head in the kitchen, so she wasn't sure what that looked like, but she was in love with the rest of the house.

It just needed interior designing. Because the only decorative item in it so far was a massive ornate mirror on the wall in the living room. Some kind of feng shui thing—reflecting the water view for peace and prosperity? She would have to look that up.

Leo was looking inscrutable as he wheeled the dining table over to her, which made her suspicious—because what was there about cakes, plates, cutlery, napkins, and glasses to warrant inscrutability?

Well, she was not going to be inscrutabilised—and she didn't *care* if that wasn't a real word! She was simply going to eat the cake, and later the pizza, like a rational woman who did not care about anything but the state of her stomach, and then drive home.

She examined the four perfectly decorated cakes. Oh, dear, she was on the cusp of a ten-kilo weight-gain.

Then she noted that Leo was pouring champagne.

'Careful—I'm fat *and* I'm driving,' she said.

'You're not fat. And driving…? We'll see.'

'Just cut the cake, Leo,' she said, not about to get into an argument so soon after she'd punched him. He couldn't *force* the champagne down her throat anyway.

Leo cut and served slices of the first cake. 'Traditional fruit cake, fondant icing.'

Sunshine took a bite. It was moist, rich, and utterly delicious. 'This one, for sure!' she said, and scooped up another forkful.

'Pace yourself. Don't vote too soon,' Leo said.

She didn't bother responding—her mouth was too full.

'You *can* have another piece, you know,' Leo offered as she scraped up a last smear of icing.

'I have to lose weight or I won't fit into my dress,' Sunshine said repressively—and then she realised the absurdity of that, given the state of her plate, and burst out laughing.

'Hey, eat as much as you want! I was just trying to protect the plate—it looked like you were trying to dig a trench in it.'

'Leo!'

He held up *I surrender* hands.

'Oh, just cut the next one,' she said, gurgling.

'Salted caramel Mark One. Pastry base covered with a film of sticky salted caramel, topped with chocolate cake layers interspersed with caramel and cream filling.'

Sunshine took a bite. Closed her eyes as flavour flooded her. She took another forkful from her plate. Sipped champagne. 'It is *so* rich and delicious.'

Leo waited while she took one more bite. Another. One more. A sip. One more. 'Finished?' he asked at last, deadpan.

Mournfully, she examined her empty plate. 'I told you I had an unhealthy interest in desserts.'

'"A shark's mouth full of sweet teeth" was how you put it.'

'It may be worse than that. It could be more like a hadrosaur's teeth. They have nine hundred and sixty—*and* they're self-sharpening!'

'What the hell is a hadrosaur?'

'A type of dinosaur.' She sighed, dispirited. 'So! I am a dinosaur—and not even a meat-eating one!'

Leo laughed so suddenly it came out as a snort.

Which made Sunshine laugh. 'Let's get onto salted caramel Mark Two before I lapse into a state of abject depression.'

'You? Abject depression while eating *cake*? That would be something to see!'

'And you will see it, I promise you, if you don't look after my hadrosauric teeth and cut me a piece of cake.'

He cut a slice and handed it over. 'Your wish, my command! Similar to Mark One, but with butterscotch cake layers.'

Sunshine ate, interspersing mouthfuls with an occasional moan of ecstasy. 'Do you have a favourite?' she asked, forking up the last mouthful. 'Because I have to tell you this is harder than I thought and I don't think I'm going to be able to choose.'

'As it turns out, I do have a favourite—but I'm not telling,' he said. 'Subliminally, knowing what I like best might sway you—maybe to deliberately pick something that is *not* my favourite—and that would never do.'

'Oh! I see what you did there! Bouncing my own words about the invitation design back at me.'

'For my next trick I will spout random facts about the mating habits of the tsetse fly.'

Sunshine laughed. 'I'm going to look that up, and next time I see you—'

'I beg you—no!' He slapped another piece of cake on her plate. 'Coconut vanilla bean cake, layered with coconut meringue butter cream.'

Sunshine stared at it, not sure if she could actually fit in another bite. But it looked so good. She picked up her fork. Ate. Sipped more champagne, then looked at her glass. 'Hey—you refilled that.'

'It was empty,' Leo explained.

Sunshine huffed, but her concentration was already moving back to her plate. One more forkful. Another. Again. Empty plate. She licked her lips, looking at the rest of the cake longingly.

'See? You didn't need to know my favourite,' Leo said. 'You decided on your own. The coconut.'

'Yes. Coconut. It would almost be *worth* getting married just to have that cake. Do you think I could have another tiny piece?'

'You can eat the whole damned cake as far as I'm concerned.'

'Dieting from tomorrow, then,' she said, holding out her plate.

Leo cut another slice. 'Don't diet, Sunshine. I like the feel of you just as you are.'

The words, the tone of his voice, made the hairs on the back of her neck stand up. 'That's...that's...immaterial. But, anyway, wh-what's your favourite?'

He smiled. A narrow-eyed smile. She didn't trust that smile.

'The fruit cake,' he said. 'But I have an idea for how we can both get our way. Compromise is my new speciality.'

Was that supposed to be meaningful? 'Both get our way with what?' she asked cautiously.

'With the cake,' Leo said, all innocence, and put the extra slice on Sunshine's plate.

He looked at her for a long moment and Sunshine saw that little tic jump to life near his mouth. She was so nervous she almost couldn't sit still. She stuck her fork into her cake, raised it to her mouth.

'And with our assignations,' Leo said smoothly.

Sunshine jerked, and the piece of cake hit her just at the corner of her bottom lip and fell.

'Two, four...there's a three in the middle,' he said, in that same dangerously soft voice.

And then, before she could string a lucid thought together, he leant in and licked the corner of her mouth.

'Just thought I'd...steal...that little drop of cream,' Leo said softly.

Dare you.

Tic-tic-tic, beside his mouth.

'I'll tell you what,' he said silkily. 'I'm going into the kitchen to organise the first compromise I was talking about. You sit here, finish your cake, look at the view, and think about the second. Think about why it is that a woman like you, who believes sex is just sex—you did say that, right?—is so freaked out by the idea that a man actually does want to have just sex with her.'

With a last piercing look at her, and a short laugh, he left the room.

And, oh, how hard it was to have her words come back to bite her. Because she had said that. Sex was just...sex.

Except that it seemed in this particular case it wasn't.

Because she was thinking about Leo too much, and caring too much, and worrying too much. The motorbike. The damned motorbike. Maybe without the motorbike they would be entwined right now on assignation three and she would be blithely uninterested in anything except his moving body parts.

So do the deal, Sunshine, and he'll get rid of the bike.

Sex twice more. Or change her name.

She touched the corner of her mouth, where he'd licked the cream, and her skin seemed to tingle.

Restless, she got to her feet, walked out onto the veranda.

'Look at the view,' he'd said.

But even that wasn't simple.

He had no idea what the view did to her. And here the beach was so disturbingly close...

She hadn't been on a beach in two years.

Leo was right: Moonbeam did have a hold over her. A hold she seemed unable to break. A hold she was too... scared...to break. Well, she would go down to the beach now and yank her *own* chain and see what happened. And

then she would tell Leo. She would tell him—she would…
God, she didn't know what she would say. Or do.

But one drama at a time.

Deep breath.

Beach.

Heart hammering, she bent to remove her shoes. Took
the first step before she could think again, kept going until
the sand was beneath her feet.

It felt strange. And good. Comforting, almost, to have
her feet sink into the sand. The scratch of salt on her face,
the roar and rush of surf sounding in her ears.

Sunshine felt her sister in the wild, careless, regal,
lovely essence of the place. Pulling at her, drawing her
closer and closer, until she was at the water's edge and the
waves were slapping at her ankles.

She let out the breath she hadn't realised she was holding on a long sigh.

This tiny private beach was it.

What she'd been looking for. Waiting to find.

Leo's beach was her sister's final resting place.

She felt tears start, and swiped a shaking hand over
her eyes.

And then she felt Leo behind her.

CHAPTER EIGHT

'I'M NOT VAIN enough to think you're crying over me, Sunshine—so why don't you tell me what the big deal is about the beach?' Leo asked.

Heartbeat. Two. Three. 'Moonbeam.'

'I thought we'd get around to Moonbeam. Everything always circles back to her.'

She turned sharply towards him. 'What's wrong with that?'

'Just the fact that she's *dead*.'

She covered her ears, gave an anguished cry, and the next thing she knew she was in his arms.

'I'm sorry. *Sorry*,' he said, and kissed her temple. 'But, Sunshine, your sister doesn't sound like the kind of person who would have wanted you to freeze, to mark time just because she wasn't there.'

'She—she wasn't. But I can't help it, Leo.'

Long moment. And then Leo said, 'So let me help you. Tell me—talk. About Moonbeam and the beach.'

She waited, shivering in his steady hold, until the urge to weep had passed, and then she pulled out of his arms and stood beside him, looking out at the horizon.

'Sunshine?'

'She told me that when she died she wanted her ashes scattered at the beach—to mix with the ocean.' She turned to look up at him. 'Why would she say that when she was so young? Do you think she knew what was going to happen?'

'I don't know, Sunshine.'

'I didn't do what she wanted. I couldn't. Can't.'

'So...where is she?'

'In an urn in my office. You were looking straight at her—that night you cooked me dinner. I was scared you'd guessed. But it was just my guilty conscience getting the better of me. Because why would you ever guess?'

'There's no need to feel guilty, Sunshine.'

'I've got my sister in an urn in my office—the exact opposite of what she wanted. What does that say about me?'

'That you're grieving.' He smoothed a windblown lock of her hair. 'You'll find a way to do what she asked. But even if you never do it won't matter to Moonbeam. It's not really Moonbeam in that urn. She's in your heart and your head. Not in the urn, Sunshine.'

She turned back to the ocean, gazing out. 'A full moon. A quiet beach. She said it would be up to me to do it on my own—no friends, no family. Just me and her.' The tears were shimmering and she desperately blinked them back. 'I think she knew how hard it would be for me. I think she knew I would take a long time. I think she didn't want to pressure me into doing anything before I was ready. I want to do it, Leo. I *do*. But...'

'Well, we have a beach,' Leo said slowly. 'And a full moon coming up. You'll be here...'

He let the words hang.

She was still. So still. And then she turned to him again. 'You wouldn't mind?' Haltingly. 'You'd let me do that?'

'Yes, I would let you. And, no, I wouldn't mind.'

'I'll...I'll think about it. I'm not sure... Not yet...'

'That's fine. The beach will always be here, and there are plenty of full moons to choose from.'

She shivered.

'You're cold,' he said. 'Come back to the house.'

She could feel him behind her as she walked across the sand and up the steps. Like a tingle inside her nerve-endings. She could feel him watching as she brushed the sand from her feet, slipped on her shoes, retied the ankle laces.

And then, 'What next?' she asked, breathless. Wanting, wanting... *What?*

But Leo merely gestured for her to go into the house.

He'd cleared the table and positioned in the middle of it a small white cardboard box with Art Deco patterning. 'Open it,' he said.

Sunshine lifted the lid to find a one-portion replica of one of the wedding cake choices. Except that on top was a decorative three-dimensional love knot formed from two men's ties.

'Compromise number one,' Leo said. 'Fruit cake—for the wedding favours. It lasts longer than the other cakes, so can be made in advance. The ties will be identical to what Caleb and Jonathan are wearing on the day.'

'Anton is a genius.' She turned to him, felt her heart stutter at the hungry look on his face. 'So! We nail the seating plan now and we're done, right?'

Leo stepped closer to her. 'That makes you happy, Sunshine, doesn't it?'

'Of—of course.'

'The fact that we've done all the planning? Or that you don't have to see me again?'

'But I *do* have to see you,' she said faintly. 'At the trial dinner.'

'You're scared of me.'

'That's...insane.'

'Prove it.'

'There's nothing to prove. And how could I prove it anyway?'

'Kiss me.'

She goggled at him. 'Excuse me?'

'You used to. Every time you saw me. Before we had sex, at least. I thought things didn't change for you just because you had sex with someone.'

'They…they don't.'

'Then kiss me hello. Or you can make it goodbye, if you want. But do it. The way you used to. Just a kiss on the cheek.'

She shook her head.

He smiled. 'Ah. So *you're* the one who won't touch now, Sunshine.'

'I—I do. I mean, I can. But it's not… I just…'

He reached out, grabbed her elbow, and she jumped back.

'See?' he said. 'What's the problem? You've stayed friends with all your exes. Why not me?'

'You're not an ex.' Her eyes widened as she realised what she'd said. 'I mean, you *are*.' Stop. Breathe. Swallow. Hair toss. 'Of course we're friends.'

'So kiss me.'

She gave an exaggerated, exasperated sigh. 'All right,' she said. She leant forward and kissed his cheek. 'There! Satisfied?'

'No. Do it again. Slower. And touch me this time. Your hand, somewhere on me.'

'Ridiculous,' she muttered.

'Just do it.'

She touched his wrist, the burn mark. 'What happened there?'

'Hot pan, don't change the subject—and that's not touching.'

'Okay—where do you want me to touch you?' she asked, rolling her eyes with great theatricality.

His eyebrows shot up. He blinked. Slowly. Again.

Seriously? He was thinking about *there*?

But, 'Improvise...' was what he said.

With the air of a person suffering a fool, and *not* gladly, she ran her fingers up his forearm. 'There.'

'Now do that and kiss me at the same time.'

'This is stupid.'

'Do it.'

Huffing out an agitated breath, Sunshine leant up and gave him a fleeting kiss on the cheek while her hand gripped his forearm.

'There! Satisfied?' she said again. Hmm. That had come out a little too breathy.

'Not good enough—you're not usually that tentative. Try again.'

She stood there, chewing her lip for a moment, and then, as though going into battle, she grabbed him by both arms and kissed him lingeringly on the cheek.

She felt the sizzle, the almost convulsive need to press into him. Jerked back. Stared. 'So!' she said, a little unsteadily.

'It's not going to work, Sunshine,' he said.

'I did it. It worked.'

'You know what I mean.'

'If you're talking about sex, I—I told you. Two times. Over. Done with. Moving on.'

He stepped closer. 'I didn't agree to two. You're not moving on—not in any sense. And I still want you.'

He looked into her eyes. She could feel the lust pulsing out of him. She could smell it. Almost taste the musky promise of it.

'You want me too,' he said. 'I can *see* it. Your eyes... You know, the size of a person's pupils is the result of a balancing act between the autonomic nervous system, which controls the fight-or-flight response, and the parasympathetic system, known for its rest and digest functions—I read that online. Another fact to add to your collection.'

He stepped closer still.

'But I prefer a simpler explanation—sexual interest in what you're looking at makes your pupils dilate. And yours, Sunshine, are looking mighty dilated.'

He pulled her into his arms, kissed her hard.

'Compromise number two, Sunshine. And assignation number three. You're not leaving here until it's done.'

CHAPTER NINE

WITHOUT WAITING FOR a response he reached for the zipper at the back of her dress and slid it down. He peeled the dress over her shoulders, down to her hips.

The dress fell to the floor and she stood there in her underwear. He'd never seen her underwear before, but wasn't surprised to find it was the sexiest in the world. Petal-pink, the same colour as her dress—and he had a sudden insight that Sunshine's underwear would always match her clothes. He'd never been a lingerie man. Until today, when he was confronted by Sunshine's wispy, lacy bra, with its tiny ribbon bows, and the matching French knickers that reminded him of a frothy strawberry dessert.

His heart was hammering wildly in his chest. He touched the bra, the knickers. 'These are staying on,' he said, and turned her to face the mirror, where they could both watch as his hands covered her breasts, caressed her through the lace, slid down her body.

When his fingers dived beneath the elastic of those gorgeous knickers he could see her eyes close, her mouth gasp open. That gap between her teeth looked so damned *hot*!

Then she threw her head back against his shoulder, opened herself to him, and he couldn't think about anything except his desperate need to have her.

'Touch me—touch me, please,' she whimpered, and his

hand slid down, between her legs, where the heat and the wetness of her almost made him come on the spot.

She orgasmed quietly—a single, sighing groan easing through her parted lips; she went so boneless she would have melted to the floor if he hadn't been holding her.

But Leo wasn't done. He kissed her ear. 'Watch,' he said, and she opened her eyes, watching in the mirror again.

He lifted her right leg slightly up and outwards, so she could see the movement of his fingers as they slid beneath the silk of her knickers.

'I love these,' he said, tugging the crotch aside a little, then dragging the waist down so she was just a little exposed, open to him.

Behind her, he smoothly, quietly, undid his jeans. Her eyes were heavy-lidded, glittering, fixed on his as he sheathed himself inside her. It was almost gentle, the way he moved—and it was a test of his control, because he was wild for her. But this time, this coupling, was all about acceptance. And so he moved slowly, stayed still inside her for long moments…and when he did move it was by infinitesimal degrees, never withdrawing from her, always there. Hands running across her skin, along the scars. Until that groaning release of hers again, when he gripped her hips and followed her, groaning her name, holding her, as the waves washed over them, unhurried, sweet, delicious.

At last she stepped away from him, bent to retrieve her dress, slid it on. She turned her back for him to zip her into it.

The he turned her to face him. Put his hands on her shoulders. 'Sunshine?' His voice had that gravelly post-coital timbre to it.

No smile. Just a haunted look unlike any he'd ever seen on her face.

'I—I'm going to go now.'

'The champagne. It's too soon to drive. You should wait.'

'I didn't want all that champagne.'

'We'll do the seating plan. Over pizza, remember?'

'The *seating* plan?' She sounded incredulous.

'I— Yes. No. Whatever you want.'

'Leo, I can't do this. I don't want to.'

'The seating plan?'

'No, not the damned seating plan. The sex. The chat. The post-coital friend routine.'

'You said you were always friends afterwards.'

'It's different. I…I care about you. And it's not kind or—or…fair to do this to me.'

'Do what?'

'Try and put me in a position where I will end up caring *more*—because that's what will happen. I don't know why you'd bother, unless it's some twisted game. Or a challenge just because I set the rules.'

'I don't play by the rules, Sunshine.'

'And I don't want to be a challenge.' She pushed tiredly at her fringe. Then squared her shoulders. 'So! I'll tell you what. You win. You come and claim your fourth time. Let's just do it. The sooner the better. And then the deal is done. Because I am not going past that.'

She could see the triumph flare in his eyes.

'Deal,' he said. 'But before we get to that I'm going to make you pizza. Then we're going to dot every *i* and cross every *t* of this wedding and get it the hell out of our relationship. And then I'm going to take you to bed and make love to you, and draw a line under assignation number three.'

She could feel her breathing quicken, her pulse start skittering, the throbbing rush between her legs.

And then Leo, smiling, added, 'But first I'm going to

read you the haiku poem your mother sent me—which I have to say I kind of liked.'

No.

No, no, no, *no*!

But it didn't seem to matter how many times she said no in her head.

Because it was there, hurting her chest, stretching her heart.

Shimmering brightly, beautifully. Overwhelming and terrifying.

She was in love with Leo Quartermaine.

It was hardly surprising that she'd fallen in love with him, Sunshine thought on her drive back to Sydney the next morning.

The best sex of her life—possibly of *anyone's* life…in the *whole history of mankind*. Meat-lovers' pizza. Tiramisu. The offer to scatter her sister's ashes a stone's throw from his house. But, really, the absolutely unfair kicker—an appreciation of her mother's haiku poetry: evidence that he was probably seriously nuts.

The eyes are sublime
Glowing without the blackness
Liberated now

What had her mother been *thinking*?

And who the hell could actually *like* that?

And how could you *not* fall in love with a guy who did?

The signs were there already that this gobsmacking love was going to be an absolute misery. She'd asked Leo to text her so that she'd know he'd got home safely—and instead of telling her not to be a lunatic Leo had smiled and said, 'Sure.'

He'd smiled! *Smiled*!

What was going to come next—checking him for cuts and scalds after a shift in the kitchen?

Er...*no*! Thank you very much.

Well, it was a new thing. Maybe it wouldn't last. Maybe they would have their fourth assignation and then, once they'd gone their separate ways, it would fade.

Except...she was already feeling a little distraught at the idea of going their separate ways.

So, no. No time to waste.

She had to take action immediately.

Their relationship had to be reversed. They had to return to the way they'd been before she'd hugged him on the couch and started this killer snowball rolling down the mountain.

They had to be friends. Just friends. Without the depth. The way they should have been all along.

Which meant no fourth assignation.

And if she didn't want to renege on their deal that meant...

Sigh.

One name-change, coming up.

To: Leo Quartermaine
From: Sunshine Smart
Subject: Loose ends
Hi Leo
Here is a copy of my name-change application. So no need for assignation number four.

The process apparently takes about four weeks. Please let me know when you've sold the bike. You will find cars are so much more convenient. Well, maybe not for parking. But think of getting around when it's raining.

I know we're all sorted for the wedding, which is great because I am up to the gills in handbags for the next week or so, but let's catch up before the trial dinner.

(Allyn) Sunshine Smart

PS: I'm assuming it's okay for me to invite a date to the trial dinner, because I owe Tony.

Leo read the note three times before it sank in.

Allyn.

She'd chosen the name-change option over more sex with him.

Well, what moron had offered her that *out?*

And then one fact pierced him like a nice, long, sharp lance between the eyes: he didn't want her to change her name for *any* reason. She was *Sunshine*. Sunshine *suited* her. Okay, he was perhaps a little unhinged, because Sunshine wasn't an appropriate name for any human being—only for dish-washing liquid—but it bloody well did suit *her*, dammit.

The second fact smacked him behind the head like one of those quintain things that swung on a pole when you hit it with your lance: maybe the sex wasn't as good for her as it was for him.

After one appalled moment he discounted that. He recognised melt-your-socks sex when he saw it, tasted it, touched it, did it.

So did she, obviously. And it scared the crap out of her.

But to go straight from his bed to the Registry of Births, Deaths and Marriages…?

Well, sorry, but that was just an insult!

He thought back to last night.

He'd read her the haiku and she had looked like some kind of wax mannequin…but then, she'd made it obvious she wasn't a haiku fan.

She'd rallied to argue with him over the remaining wedding preparations. Par for the course.

She'd eaten the pizza as though it were going to be her last earthly meal—no surprises there.

Dinnertime conversation had been as peculiar as usual,

with Sunshine imparting strange but true facts. Leonardo Da Vinci had invented scissors—*who knew?*—there was a maze in England shaped like a Dalek—*how cool was that?*—forest fires moved faster uphill than downhill, and the crack in a breaking glass moved faster than three thousand miles per hour.

Then they'd had more amazing sex, using tiramisu in ways that would make it his favourite dessert for eternity.

And this morning she'd kissed him goodbye. On the mouth. As though she did it every day. And he'd *liked* that.

She'd asked him to text her when he got home. And he'd *done* it—*happily.*

So…*what?* Now he was supposed to accept that it was all over?

And what was the deal with *let's catch up before the trial dinner?*

Was she freaking *kidding* him? He was not *catching up* with her. Unless it was to bang her brains out in assignation number four.

Did she think he didn't know when he was being friend-zoned?

He *wasn't* going to be friend-zoned by Sunshine Smart.

He was not Gary or Ben or Iain or Tony—relegated to coffee catch-ups, Facebook status updates, and being taken to dinner to check people's hair-length.

He was *not* her freaking friend.

His brain felt as if it were foaming with rage.

He would email her telling her he would *not* be catching up with her before the trial dinner. And when he saw her at the trial dinner he would drag her aside and force her to tell him that she—

His brain stuttered to a halt there.

Tell him that she…that she…

That she…

Into his head popped a picture of her kissing him good-bye that morning.

Asking him to text her when he got home.

That she…

That *he*…

Oh, my God.

All or nothing. Off the cliff. Into the abyss.

She was the one.

She would fight tooth and nail not to be, but that was what she was.

The one.

And Leo had no idea what to do about it.

It's hemp, Jim, but not as we know it.

Leo had done a double-take the moment he'd seen Sunshine.

Hemp was not sexy.

Everyone knew that.

So why did the sight of Sunshine Smart wearing it make him want to drool?

A simple loose ankle-length column of dark bronze—and, God, he'd love to see her underwear in *that* colour—with two tiny straps fastened at the shoulders in untie-me-please bows. She'd left off the lipstick as well as the eye-goop and looked fresh as a sea breeze. Her hair was loose. Towering heels in gold. Gold drop earrings, straight as arrows, pointing to those mind-game bows. She also had a thick gold cuff clasped around one arm, just above the elbow. But she never wore jewellery…

Well, obviously she does *sometimes, imbecile.*

Yep. A hundred and fifty guests to feed, and he was pondering Sunshine's jewellery-wearing habits. *Great.*

He strode over to her. 'Sunshine.'

'Allyn,' she corrected.

'Not yet, though, right? And—' he turned to the guy

who had popped up beside her like a cork in a pool '—you must be Tony. Let me show you to your table.'

Leo led them to their seats, introduced them to the others at their table.

And then... Well, her fringe was getting long. She'd brushed it aside—training it for the wedding, he figured—but one piece had sprung back over her forehead. He smoothed it back to where it was supposed to be.

Her gorgeous eyes widened. He heard her quick intake of breath, saw the daze in her eyes. It felt like a 'moment'—one of those bubble-like moments where everything was right with the world.

He sensed Tony watching him. Everyone else at the table too.

Good, he thought savagely. *I'm marking my territory, people, and she belongs to me.*

It had been two weeks since Sunshine had seen Leo—two weeks in which the only contact he'd made had come in the form of three niggardly emails: one rebuffing her suggestion that they catch up before tonight—which had hit her like a blow—the second a message about wines for the wedding, with the most *casual* mention that he'd sold his bike and bought a 'nice safe Volvo'—how dared he be casual about that?—and the third with details of tonight's trial dinner. She suspected it was the same email he'd sent to all guests, except that to hers he'd added, *Don't forget to bring your sister.*

With so little encouragement to pine for him, and fewer reasons to worry about him now that he was *sans* motorbike, Sunshine figured she should have managed to get her wayward emotions under control. But the bike sale hadn't seemed to lessen her anxiety over him. She thought, and thought, and thought about him. *All the goddamned time.* Exactly what she'd been trying to avoid.

And then that one touch of his, brushing her fringe aside, and her emotions had surged so suddenly she'd almost thrown herself at him.

Now just the sight of him walking to the middle of the restaurant and clapping his hands to get everyone's attention, looking so delicious in that crisp white jacket, started her stomach jumping like popping candy.

He made a welcome speech—explained what would happen, ran through the menu, asked people to make sure they passed on all feedback, good and bad—and all through it Sunshine stared at him as though he were a nice big bowl of tiramisu...

When he left for the kitchen the whole night suddenly felt flat—and it didn't reshape itself except when he made his occasional forays from the kitchen to take a momentarily empty seat and chat to guests.

But never at Sunshine's table. And she didn't know whether to be happy about that or not. On the one hand she wouldn't have had to strain every minuscule cilia in her ears, trying to hear what he was saying. But on the other he'd surely notice that she had become, in just two weeks, the equivalent of a fried bat.

And then he was at the table next to hers, and Sunshine caught his eyes on her for the first time since he'd shown her to her table.

The hairs on the back of her neck stood up. She couldn't breathe. Couldn't think. Couldn't even seem to swallow. He was nodding at something the woman next to him was saying but he was looking at Sunshine.

After ignoring her for two whole weeks he was daring to look at her as if he would drag her off to a corner, rip off her clothes and—

His head jerked to the side, towards the entrance, and Sunshine's eyes jerked reflexively. There was a disturbance going down, being played out in a series of split-seconds.

An escalating pitch of voice. A scuffling sound. A shift of bodies. And—

Natalie Clarke. *Uh-oh.*

Within seconds Leo was up and walking swiftly over to Natalie, taking her arm, murmuring to the restaurant manager who'd been trying to handle the situation, and escorting Natalie out onto the viewing platform.

Sunshine felt a little as she had that night at the Rump & Chop Grill. Light-headed with fury on Leo's behalf... desperate to protect him. She didn't even wait for her head to tell her heart it was none of her business. With a fixed smile and an incoherent murmur about a 'wedding issue', Sunshine took off after Leo.

CHAPTER TEN

SUNSHINE REACHED THE viewing platform just in time to see Natalie land a swinging slap against Leo's cheek.

The burst of rage that flared in her head made her shake. 'What the *hell's* going on?' she demanded, grabbing Natalie's hand as it drew back for a second go.

'Go back inside, Sunshine,' Leo said, and tried to shove her behind him.

'You!' Natalie said contemptuously. 'Choke-girl! *You're* the Sunshine person?' She looked Sunshine up and down. 'They say at Q Brasserie that he's besotted with you. But he doesn't know *how* to love someone. He's not capable. He can't even *touch* you.'

Sunshine didn't bother answering. She simply manoeuvred herself beside Leo—which required a sharp nudge with her elbow, since he seemed determined to keep her out of harm's way—and then took his hand in hers, brought it to her lips, kissed it, rubbed it against her cheek.

'Really?' she asked Natalie, with a raise of her eyebrows.

Surrendering, Leo drew Sunshine protectively against his side. 'Natalie,' he said, 'tonight is a private function. And there are journalists inside who are probably wondering what the hell's going on out here. Can we *not* play this out in a blaze of publicity? Go back to Sydney—or there's a hotel nearby if you don't feel up to driving back tonight.'

'Why don't I go and wait at your house, Leo?' Natalie purred the question, shrugging out of her coat. She shimmied a little, sinuous as a snake.

Sunshine, beset by another burst of rage, stiffened, and Leo squeezed her hand slightly. Telling her to let it go.

And she should. She knew she should…

But Natalie licked her lips and raised one eyebrow, and the rage consumed her.

Sunshine laughed—a brittle laugh that sounded nothing like her. 'I'd forgotten about the tattoos,' she said. 'Butterflies. They're the gang rapists of the insect world, you know.'

She heard Leo choke on a laugh and she squeezed *his* hand. Hard.

Natalie fluttered one arm out to look at her tattoos. 'Don't be ridiculous.'

'They are so desperate to mate they perch on a female pupa—that's the metamorphosis stage, you know, where they go from larva to—'

'This is disgusting.'

'I *know*!' Wide-eyed. 'Especially because they perch there in a pack and wait for the female to emerge. And she's still limp, and her wings haven't even opened, and the first male just kind of grabs her and…well, you get the picture. And then the others take their turn.'

'That's…' Words seemed to fail Natalie.

Sunshine was contemplating Natalie's arms sadly. 'Next time get an eagle; at least they mate for life.'

Natalie stood there, quivering with impotent rage, staring from Sunshine to Leo.

One fraught moment. Another. Three people on one small viewing platform. Nobody moving.

And then, with a last look of loathing at Sunshine, Natalie turned on her heel and stalked off the platform.

Sunshine dropped Leo's hand and stepped back. '*Now* I'll go back in,' she said.

'Why did you even come out?'

'I just…I just thought you might need some support.'

'It looked a little like a leap into the abyss to me.'

No. *No!* 'I just don't like violence. And she slapped you. It made me…mad.' She looked at his face, which was still reddened where Natalie's hand had connected.

Half-laugh as he ran his fingers over his cheek. 'Yeah, you'll have to lift some weights if you want to match her.'

Sunshine, conscience-stricken, felt the colour drain from her face. 'Oh, my God, you're right. I'm just like her.'

Leo took her hands in his, pulled her towards him. 'You're nothing like her.'

'But I punched you!'

'And then you kissed it better, remember?'

'I— Yes, I remember.'

She shivered.

'Are you cold?

Nod. 'I brought a coat, but it's in my car.'

'Then come here,' he said softly, and drew her in, folding his arms around her. 'And Moonbeam? Is she in the car too?'

She nodded again.

'So it's happening?' he asked gently.

Another nod. 'Yes, if you're sure you don't mind.' And then, just a whisper, 'Tomorrow is the anniversary of… of…'

'Ah, Sunshine.' He stroked his hand over her hair and they stayed like that for a long moment. 'We'll disappear as soon as dessert is cleared, okay?'

'Tony…'

'Yeah—I don't give a rat's ass about Tony, and neither do you.'

'I don't think rats' asses are an apt comparison.'

'A horse's ass, then.'

She giggled, and then buried her face against his chest to stifle it. Because it wasn't funny.

'Whatever he is, he can fend for himself,' Leo said. 'Because I know he didn't drive down with you. Aside from anything else, I know you wouldn't have him in the car with Moonbeam.'

'How do you know that?'

'Because I just do.' Slight pause. 'So that stuff about butterflies—was it true?'

'Well, it's true of *certain* species,' Sunshine said, drawing slowly out of his arms. 'I'm not sure about *all* species.'

He opened the door to the restaurant, laughing. 'Poor Natalie. Probably *not* arms full of rapists.'

'Do you think I should tell her?' Sunshine asked, feeling suddenly guilty.

'If I could find pupil dilation on the internet I'm sure Natalie can find rapist butterflies,' Leo said. 'I like the thing about the eagles, though. Mating for life.'

It was time.

Sunshine was standing on his veranda at the top of the stairs, barefoot, with the urn in her arms. She was wearing a long knitted garment over her hemp dress. It flowed down to her ankles. No fastenings. A little bit witchy, a little bit hippie—perfect for a ceremonial ash-tossing.

'Right,' she said, and stood there looking irresolute.

Leo simply waited.

'Right,' she said again, with a tiny nod this time. And then she shot a look at Leo over her shoulder. 'I have to do this myself.'

'I know. I'll come down to the beach, just in case you need me, but I'll stay at the base of the steps.'

'I won't need you.'

'In case.' Implacable.

She looked paler than usual. Tense. And oddly hopeful.

And then she straightened her shoulders and started down the steps.

Leo waited two minutes, then followed. By the time he reached the sand her toes were in the wash.

He knew he would never forget the image of Sunshine, alone, surrounded by moon, surf, sand, night, as she lifted the urn to her face, kissed it.

And then she took off the lid and threw it behind her, discarded.

As if on cue an offshore breeze stirred, and Sunshine threw her head back, hugging the urn to her chest for one brief moment. Then, in one sudden, decisive movement, she threw the ashes up and out towards the water. She repeated the move once more. Then she bent, filled the urn with the seawater rushing in, waited while the water receded, then raced in again…tipped the urn so its contents hit the sand just as the new wave broke. And the last of Moonbeam's ashes were carried out to the ocean.

The minutes ticked by.

The breeze died away.

The rhythmic whooshing of surf on sand continued.

Life goes on.

And then Sunshine tossed that beautiful urn aside as though it were nothing but a broken shard of shell and walked back up the beach towards him, silent, tears streaming.

He opened his arms and she walked right into them. He said nothing. Just held her as her tears gradually eased, then stopped.

Staying in the circle of his arms, she looked up. 'Thank you,' she said. 'You know, she would have loved you.'

And you? he wanted to ask. But instead he said, 'Come to bed, Sunshine.'

She looked at his face in the moonlight. Touched his cheek. Nodded. 'One last time.'

She woke wearing one of Leo's shirts, alone on the mattress.

The makeshift curtains were drawn, except for a crack through which a piercing sliver of light beamed.

She got out of bed to tug the curtains back—and there it was: Moonbeam's beach. Wild and beautiful and… peaceful. Perfect.

Leo wandered in, wearing unbuttoned jeans and a navy blue T-shirt.

And the feeling of peace evaporated as her stomach started its usual Leo-induced cha-cha.

Time for reality.

'I'm about to make you an omelette,' he said, smiling. 'It will only be a few minutes, if you want to come out on the veranda when you're ready. And don't worry—there will be chorizo in there.'

A dart of panic stabbed her. 'No. I don't want it.'

'Don't like chorizo?'

'It's not about the ingredients.'

The smile vanished. 'Then what is it about?'

'The fact that you never cook for people.'

'And yet I do it for you.'

Her breath hitched. 'But I—I don't want you to cook for me.'

'Why not?'

'Because it's not what you do. You shouldn't change for me. Because…'

'Because…?'

'Because I can't change for you.'

'I haven't asked you to.'

'Oh.' That took the wind out of her sails. 'That's…good. I was scared because…'

'Because?'

'Well, Natalie said last night the people at Q Brasserie…they think you're besotted with me. That wouldn't be good.'

'I'm not besotted,' he said. 'Does that reassure you?'

'Yes. No. I don't know.'

'Multiple *choice*, Sunshine? How…comprehensive.'

'No. I mean—yes, it reassures me,' she said. 'I just… want us to be on the same page.'

'What specific page are you talking about?'

'Page number four,' she said. 'Four assignations. All settled. And I'm glad we did it. I was feeling guilty because you gave up your bike, and I never got around to filing the papers to change my name—because it didn't feel right, somehow. And I still…owed you.'

'Is that what last night was about? Honouring the deal?'

Last night came rushing back at her—the gentleness and joy of it. The way he'd hovered over her, lavishing her with his touch. Hands so sure and wonderful. The layered feelings of his mouth sliding over her, sometimes gentle, sometimes demanding. Worshipping her body with his— that's what it had felt like. Whenever she'd made a sound he'd been there, kissing her, soothing her. And even when she'd made no sound he'd been just there—something of his, on her.

But now, the morning after, with the terror of love choking her, she wanted to throw herself at his feet and beg him never to go, never to die.

But he couldn't promise that.

'Yes,' she whispered. 'I owed you and now we're done.'

She snatched her dress off the floor and started walking away.

'Where are you going?' Leo asked

'To the bathroom. To change.'

Leo folded his arms over his chest. 'Not only have my

eyes been all over your body, but so have my hands and my mouth. And now you're running to the bathroom?'

She paused, undecided. And then, with a defiant shrug, she ripped off the shirt she was wearing, dragged her dress over her head.

Leo bent, scooped something off the floor. 'Forgetting these?' he asked.

She snatched the tiny bronze-coloured panties from him and struggled into them while trying to stay covered.

'There,' she said. 'Happy?'

He watched her, brooding, hooded. 'No.'

'Leo, what do you want from me?'

'I want to know where you think we go from here—one month out from the wedding.'

'Well, we're going to be family. Sort of...'

'I'm not your brother.'

'I meant more like...like surrogate family. Like friends.'

'I'm not your friend.'

'But we *could* be friends.'

'I told you way back when that I don't do that.'

'I know you don't, usually—but I'm not like your other exes.'

'And I'm not like yours. I won't be Facebook "friend-ing" you, making it to a movie, popping out for a coffee, or catching up over a casual dinner where we give each other a kiss on the cheek goodnight.'

'But why not?'

'Because I want you.'

She stared helplessly at him as her heart thudded in her aching chest. 'You already said you *didn't* want me.'

'I didn't say that.'

'You said you weren't besotted.'

'That's different. I want you, all right...the same way you want me. And it's got nothing to do with friendship.'

She swallowed. God. God, God, *God.* 'I—I don't want to…to want you like that.'

He moved like lightning, grabbing her arms and hauling her up on her toes. 'But you do. Your pupils are telling me you do, Sunshine,' he said, and smiled. 'Nice and big—for me.' He nudged his pelvis against her. 'Like that—nice and big. For you.'

She swallowed convulsively. 'You know I can't let myself love you.' The words sounded torn from her throat.

'Who mentioned love? Not me—*you* did, Sunshine. You.' He kissed her, a hard, drugging, wrenching scorch of mouth and tongue that made her melt and steam and long for him.

She almost cried out a protest when he stopped.

'Call this thing between us anything you want—except friendship,' he said. 'Because I will *never* be your friend.'

He let her go suddenly, and she stumbled backwards.

'I'm giving you fair warning, Sunshine: I *will* have you again. Five, six, seven times. Or ten, twenty. Anything except four. I will have you again, and there will be nothing friendly about it.'

Frustrated and furious, Leo went down to the beach after Sunshine had left.

No—she hadn't 'left'; she had run away, as if all the demons of hell were after her.

He needed a swim to snap his tortured brain back to a modicum of intelligence. And he hoped the water was frigid. He hoped—

Oh.

Oh, God.

There, a metre from the water, skewed in the sand, was the urn Sunshine had tossed aside last night.

And it was more effective than a swim in frigid water ever could have been.

Because it brought back every heartbreaking moment of that scene on the beach as the woman he loved had finally found the courage to say goodbye to her sister. The way she had given herself to him so sweetly afterwards, with gentleness and acceptance and yearning, and a heated desire that had seemed insatiable.

The contrast to this morning was not pretty.

He ran his hands over his head. Today was the anniversary of Moonbeam's death. And what had he done? Pushed and pushed her, without even giving her a chance to think. All but demanding that she strip for him, forcing her to kiss him, telling her he would take whatever he wanted, when he wanted.

It had been his survival instinct—alive and kicking—telling him to go his own way, *get* his own way, no matter what *she* wanted.

But seeing the urn was a concrete reminder that his way was not hers.

She had taken two years to farewell the sister she adored. She wasn't ready to love anyone else. Was too scared of the pain of it and too guilt-stricken to reach for what her sister could never have.

And he didn't have the right to force the love from her.

Not the right, and not the power.

She didn't want him to have all of her, the way he craved.

And if she couldn't give him her all, he was going to have to find a way to settle for nothing.

CHAPTER ELEVEN

'*I WILL HAVE you again, and there will be nothing friendly about it.*'

Those words had been going around and around in Sunshine's head incessantly for four long weeks, until she'd started to wonder if she'd be too scared to go to the wedding.

She hadn't even been able to pluck up the courage to go to the airport to meet Jon's flight, because she was so certain Leo would be there—ready either to pounce on her or ignore her, and she didn't know which would be worse.

Now she'd finally got to see Jonathan, he didn't waste time on small talk. She barely had time to slap a Campari into his hand as he took a seat on her couch before he fixed his eagle eye on her across the coffee table and asked, 'What's going on with Leo, Sunshine?'

'What do you mean?

'Only that you went from mentioning his name in your emails to the point where I wanted to vomit to complete radio silence a month ago. And he did the same to Caleb.'

'Oh.'

'Yes, *oh*. I did warn you it wouldn't be hands across the water singing "Kumbaya" at the end.'

'Strictly speaking, that's hands around the campfire.'

'I will build a campfire and throw you on it if you give

me internet facts in the middle of this discussion. What happened?'

'It was the four-times rule.'

Jon rolled his eyes. 'Yes?'

'I wanted to stop at two, because I was…liking him too much, I guess. And he didn't want to stop.'

'But you stopped anyway?'

'Well…no. I couldn't seem to resist.'

'And the problem is… ?'

'That I just… I can't stop. Wanting him, I mean.'

'So *have* him.'

'You know I can't do that.'

'What I know, Sunny, is that you tell yourself a lot of crap! How do you know it's too painful to love a man when you've never done it? And don't hide behind the four-times rule. It's easy for you to pretend you've always stopped at one or two or even none because you're scared of caring too much. But the truth is you stop because you don't care *enough*! Which brings me back to Leo and the fact that you obviously finally *do* care enough. *What* is the problem?'

'I'm scared.'

'Sunny—love *is* scary. Not just for you, for everyone.'

'He doesn't love me. He only *wants* me.'

'So make him love you.'

'You can't make someone love you.'

'The Sunshine Smart *I* know can—if she wants to.'

'Well, she *doesn't* want to.'

'Just think about it.'

'No.'

'Then I'm telling your mother you asked for a book of original haiku poems for Christmas.'

She sputtered out a laugh. 'You're a rat, Jonathan.'

'Pour me another Campari and get me the computer. I'm going to look up Sydney's hottest models and try to choose Leo's next girlfriend. And when he nails her I am going to hire a skywriter to scrawl "I TOLD YOU SO" over Bondi Beach.'

And then Jonathan left his seat, came over to her, lifted her onto his lap. 'Sunny, darling one, give yourself a break and grab him.'

'How can I when…when Moonbeam…?'

'Moonbeam! *Sunny.* God, Sunny! Is *that* what this is about? She can't have love so you won't? She never wanted you to throw yourself onto her funeral pyre. That is so *not* her. And reverse the situation—would you have wanted *her* to give up living?'

'No. Of course not! And I know she would have loved him…and that makes it easier. If only…'

'If only?'

'If only he would never die,' she said, and buried her face against his chest.

'Oh, Sunny.' Jon kissed the top of her head. 'Would it really hurt any less just because you're not together? Wouldn't that be worse?'

'It's so hard. *Too* hard.'

'Yeah, life's hard. So why make it harder?'

Sipping a gin and tonic, Caleb leant back in his chair and examined his brother, head on one side.

It reminded Leo of Sunshine's curious bird look. And he couldn't bear it. He surged to his feet and paced the room, trying to shed some of the nervous energy that had infiltrated his body as the countdown to the wedding—to when he would see Sunshine again—began.

'Now that it's just us, suppose you tell me what's going on with Sunshine?' Caleb suggested.

'Nothing.'

'What happened? Did she fall in love with you and you had to hurt her feelings?'

Silence as Leo slid into his seat, picked up his drink and took a long swallow.

'Well?' Caleb prompted. And then his gaze sharpened. 'Oh, boy.'

'"Oh, boy"—*what*?'

'It was the other way around. You fell in love with *her*, and she had to hurt *your* feelings.'

'Not exactly.'

'Blood from a stone, or what?'

Leo put down his drink, ran his hands through his three centimetres of hair. 'We had an agreement—sex only. Four times.'

Caleb nodded, understanding. 'The four-times rule.'

Leo shot a startled look at Caleb. 'You *know* about that?'

'Yep. And you obviously agreed to it. Idiot. So then what?'

'And then she wanted…less.'

'She wanted less. Why? You were no good in the sack? Because that's not what I've heard.'

'Because she didn't want to care about me. Not just me—about anyone.'

'That is the dumbest thing ever.'

'It's a long story that I'm not going to go into except to say that she's not looking for romantic attachments. She only wants to be friends. But I pushed it. I pushed and pushed until I got all four times. But it didn't work. '

Caleb choked on his drink. 'She didn't *friend*-zone you!'

'She tried. I refused.' Deep sigh. 'And I ended up with nothing.'

Caleb was staring at him, flabbergasted. 'You are one dumb bastard.'

'Thank you,' Leo said dryly, and jumped to his feet again, pacing.

'So what are you going to do?' Caleb asked.

'Get through the wedding. Try to accept it's over.'

'That's not the Leo Quartermaine I know.'

'She was up-front from day one and I should have accepted it. The thing with her sister—it was devastating for her. I should have understood and left her alone, but I…' Stop. Start again. 'Instead I pushed her and pushed her.' Stop. Start again. 'And what right do I have to push her into feeling something she's not ready for?'

'We're never ready—none of us—for love.'

'She didn't fall in love with me. She wouldn't let herself.'

'So change her mind.'

Leo came to a stop in front of Caleb. 'She won't do it. She says that she would be anguished in love—live for him, die for him. That's the only way for her to love.' He stared at his brother. 'And I don't think I…'

'You don't think you…?'

'Deserve it. Deserve *her*. All I could say to her the last time I saw her was that I would *not* be her friend, that I would have her again—and again, and again—and that she couldn't stop me.' He was shaking now. 'That's the kind of thing someone like Natalie would want to hear, not Sunshine. The Natalie Clarkes are for me, not the Sunshine Smarts.'

A hopeless, helpless shrug.

'And she ran for the door faster than you could blink. And then I went down to the beach and I saw the urn and it hit me—what she'd been through the night before, when all I'd wanted was to help her find peace. But that morning…the anniversary…I was pushing her because I wanted more.' He scrubbed his hands over his face. 'No wonder she ran away from me.'

Three paces away. Three back.

'As soon as I saw the urn, Caleb, I knew that she would never belong to someone who's clawed and scraped his way out of hell, who's learned to grab and take and steal. Well,

I won't steal from *her*. I mean, who am I to steal from her what she doesn't want to freely give? Why would I think I'm special enough to—?' Stop. Start again. 'Who am I to even *want* it?'

Caleb stood slowly. 'Who are *you*, Leo? Just the bravest, best, most wonderful—' He broke off, grabbed Leo in a fierce hug.

For long moments they clung together. And then Caleb drew back, tears in his eyes.

'Now, I don't pretend to know the significance of the urn. But I know this: you deserve *everything*. And I'm going to give you an argument that will appeal to the noble, valiant, chivalrous, gallant core of you that our pathetic parents did *not* manage to destroy, no matter what you think.'

He gripped Leo by the shirtfront, looking fiercely into his eyes.

'You know why you deserve her? Because you will look after her better than any other man on the planet. Because you will live for *her*, die for *her*. How will you forgive yourself if some substandard joker breaks down her defences—someone who *won't* live and die for her? Who won't throw himself into that freaking abyss you carp on and on about? Think about that, Leo. Think about *that*.'

Leo stared at his brother.

And then he smiled.

CHAPTER TWELVE

THE WEDDING DAY was perfection.

It was warm, the sun was shining, and the restaurant sparkled.

A romantic day. A glorious day.

A day for *not* throwing yourself at the drop-dead gorgeous man that you were head over ears in love with. Even if every hair on your body tingled the moment you saw him stepping onto the terrace in shoes *you'd* designed, as if he owned the world and knew exactly what to do with it.

Even if you wanted to run your fingers through his newly grown hair and slide your hands over the lapels of his sharp and sexy suit, to lean in and take the clean, soapy smell of him into your brain via your nasal cavity.

Sunshine had thought getting her first Leo sighting out of the way would take the pressure off her, but it seemed to have had the opposite effect. Every one of her senses had sprung to life and seemed to crave something that could be found only in his immediate orbit.

Despite her wildly thumping heart and her clammy hands she tried to look serene as she made her way around the terrace, greeting, smiling, chatting. Her parents were looking as deliriously happy as usual. They'd brought Leo a batch of carob and walnut cookies. And a homemade diary for next year. And a haiku poem, framed, as a thank-you for inviting them to the beach that morning to see Moonbeam's final resting place.

They'd told her that he'd loved everything, that he was wonderful. She'd thought for an insane moment they intended to adopt him!

Sunshine was wondering whether to apologise to him about the framed haiku—at least it would be a valid reason to approach him—when, amazingly, she saw him go over to her parents. The three of them looked like a secret club as they whispered together, and then Leo was enfolded in her mother's arms and hugged almost convulsively. And then her father hugged him. The three of them were laughing, looking so *right* together. And then Leo kissed her mother on the cheek, shook her father's hand in a two-handed grip, and moved away.

Oh, my God. How the hell was she supposed to fall out of love with a man who was like *that* with her parents?

He really, *really* must like haiku!

There was just one thing left on Leo's wedding to-do list: make Sunshine fall in love with him before the cake-cutting.

Caleb was sure he could do it. Jonathan had threatened him with violence if he didn't at least try. And even her parents had given him a few pointers.

But he knew she was going to be a tough nut to crack.

Watching her do the rounds in that glistening, shimmering, silver dress, practically floating in those amazing shoes, he had felt his heart both soar and ache.

She'd painted her nails silver, and was wearing glittery earrings and a matching ring in addition to the swinging sun and moon chain. Her hair was perfect—even the fringe was behaving itself. She was wearing a slick of eyeliner;

she'd told him she would way back, when they'd struck their deal, so it was allowed. And deep rose lipstick.

Gorgeous, gorgeous, *gorgeous*.

Five times he'd tried to approach her. Five times he'd lost his nerve.

The upshot was that by the time everyone was seated they hadn't spoken a word to each other. Not one word.

But he nevertheless felt as connected to her as a piano wire to its tuning pin—he was sure if they just got the tension right the music would soar. How poetic was that?

He was aware of every mouthful she ate during dinner, and every mouthful she didn't. He heard every laugh. Caught every quickly averted look from those miraculous eyes whenever he glanced in her direction.

And then Jon and Caleb were moving to the small podium. Standing there, holding hands. Leo started to panic.

Time was almost up.

Jonathan cleared his throat, tapped his glass, and Sunshine held her breath as all eyes turned to the newlyweds.

'It's *that* time of the evening,' Jonathan said. 'All of you here tonight are close to one of us—and hence to both of us. You've shared our journey. You know our story. We are so happy to be home, to be here, to be with you. So happy that we don't intend to bore you to death with speeches! All we want to do is share with you the vows we spoke to each other last week in New York.

'They're short vows—but the words are very important to us. So…here goes: *Caleb, you are the one. When I look in your eyes I see my yearning…and the truth. When you smile at me I know I can tell you anything and find everything. When we touch I feel it in every breath, every nerve, every heartbeat. When we kiss it is magic and delight. And home as well. When you laugh, when you cry, when you rage, and even when you sneer—because you sure can sneer—I am with you. You are everything to me and always will be. Caleb, my one, this is my vow to you.'*

Caleb blinked hard.

'Oh,' he said. 'That's the second time—and it gets me just as much as it did the first time. My turn: *My Jonathan. I have known love before. Friends, colleagues. Most importantly brother—and off-script, because Jon won't mind, Leo, by God, you know how important you are to me— but never before this love. This love is wrenching. Lovely. Scared. Careful. Proud. This love calms me. Excites me. Reassures me. Delights me. This love is everything. This love—my love—I will not and cannot be without. This love I give back to you—you will never be without it. Jonathan, this is my vow to you.'*

Sunshine, her breath caught somewhere in her chest, felt an acrid sting at the back of her nose. Tears. She was going to cry.

Because *she* wanted that kind of love. *Wanted* it. *So* much.

Leo had told her a month ago that he would not be her friend, that she would come to him. But she had been too scared. And now it was too late. Because Leo hadn't even spoken to her—had barely looked at her today. And she was *still* too scared.

She walked quickly towards the entrance, smiling, eyes full of tears. Four steps away. Three. Two. One—

Her arm was grabbed. She was spun around. And Leo was there. Unsmiling.

'What is it, Sunshine?' he asked. 'Did it hit you? Finally? That it's what you want?'

'I can't, Leo.'

'Enough! I've had *enough*, Sunshine. You damned well *can*. I'm lonely without you. I need you.'

Her heart ached, throbbed. But she shook her head.

He ignored the head-shake, took her hand, dragged her to the ladies' restroom.

'A restroom?' she asked. 'We're going to have this discussion in a restroom?'

'Oh, it's not just a restroom,' he said. 'It's a restroom with custom-made blue and green toilet paper.'

She stared at him. 'With…?' She whirled. Raced into one of the cubicles. Laughed.

He'd followed her in and she turned. 'Why?' she asked.

'Because I love you,' he said.

'What kind of juxtaposition is that? Toilet paper and love?' She could hear the breathiness in her voice. *Oh, God—oh, my God. Is this happening?*

'The toilet paper is a big deal, Sunshine. A *very* big deal. Because I said I'd never do it—and yet I did. People can do that, you know. Say they'll never do something and then do it. Like fall in love when they say they have no room in their hearts.'

'You s-said…you t-told me…you were not—*not*—besotted with me.'

'I'm *not* besotted with you. Besotted is for amateurs. I'm madly, crazily, violently in love with you. It's not the same thing. We're talking a massive abyss, no parachute.'

She swallowed. 'Leo, I—I…'

'Think about it,' he urged, stepping closer. 'You suck at making lists—I excel. Complementary.'

Impossible laughter. Choked off. 'Romantic,' she said.

'You do your best work at night, and so do I. So we're synchronised.'

'*Very* romantic.'

'You know stupid stuff and I want to hear it.'

She slapped a hand over her mouth, swallowing the giggle.

'You eat,' he said, starting to smile. 'I cook.'

'Hmm…'

'Getting closer, am I? Because I will cook for you morning, noon, and night—sending people all over Sydney into a state of shock! I will name a cut of meat after you. I will teach you to cook paella. I will invent a five-course degustation dessert menu just so I can watch you devour sugar.'

Half-laugh, half-tears. 'Oh, Leo.'

'I will play *"Je t'aime-ich liebe-ti amor You Darling"* in the bedroom.'

'You will not!' she said.

'That was a trick one. But you can *decorate* the bedroom. The bamboo is ordered, just in case you want a Balinese honeymoon suite, but you can do it any way you want. Perhaps go easy on the pink, though. And— Look, don't you *get* it? Do I really have to keep going?'

She was almost breathless. Staring. Hoping. Wanting this—him. 'What do I have to do in return?'

He grabbed her hand, flattened it against his heart. 'You get the easy bit. All you have to do is love me.'

She looked into his eyes. Knew that there still wasn't any room in her heart—because he'd taken up every bit of it.

'That's too easy. Because I already do love you.' Her eyes widened. 'Oh, my God, I said it. I love you. I've jumped. No parachute.'

He closed his eyes, took a deep breath. Opened them. So serious. 'I have a very particular kind of love in mind. I have to belong. To you. I have to *belong* to you, Sunshine.'

'I know,' she said. 'You want me to throw myself off the cliff. Sink into that damned abyss. Pour my soul into you and drown in you so that you are everything. Live for you, die for you. Too easy, I'm telling you!'

He let her hands go to pull her into his arms, kissed her mouth. 'And I want you to look at our beach and know that your sister is at peace, and that I am always with you to bear whatever grief you have.'

She was crying now, and he was wiping her tears with his thumbs.

'And children,' he said. 'I want a daughter named Amaya Moonbeam.'

More tears. 'Oh, Leo.'

'And a second daughter who can take on Allyn. And a son named whatever the hell you want. Only perhaps not Oaktree or Thunderbolt or Mountain.'

How could you laugh and cry at the same time? 'I can manage that.'

He kissed her again. 'And shoes. I want custom-made shoes. I'm not wearing any other kind from now on.'

'Well, that goes without saying.'

'And maybe a weekly haiku.'

'Um—no! We are *not* encouraging my mother in that.'

'Okay. But your parents get their own wing in the beach house, so they can be close to their daughters any time they want and teach me how to be the kind of parent who brings up wonderful kids.'

Crying hard. 'Leo!'

'And I still want you to change your name. But only your surname—to make you mine, Sunshine Quartermaine. With a ten-tier coconut vanilla bean wedding cake to seal the deal.'

Sunshine sighed and leant into him. Kissed him so hard his heart leapt. 'The medulla oblongata,' she said, rubbing her hand over his heart.

He felt the laugh building. 'The what?'

'The part of the brain that controls the heartbeat,' she said.

'God, I love you,' he said. 'So! Let's go and give the old medulla oblongata a real workout. Because what I really, really want right now, Sunshine, is assignation number five. And tomorrow morning we'll go for number six. And I— God, someone's coming in. What the *hell* are we doing in a restroom? Let's blow this joint.'

* * * * *